His Toughest Call

His Toughest Call

A Pytheon Security Romance

Joss Wood

His Toughest Call

Tule Publishing First Printing, December 2017

The Tule Publishing Group, LLC

ISBN: 978-1-948342-01-8

Chapter One

SETH HALCOTT LIFTED a glass of whiskey to his mouth and, out of the corner of his eye, saw the whisk of a wedding dress, the hint of dark fingers clamped around an ultra-feminine wrist. He leaned backwards on his barstool to look through the frosted glass of doors of the hotel bar to the lobby beyond and, yep, that definitely looked like a bride being hustled out of the hotel by a bulky policeman.

Seth released a low curse, tossed his whisky back, and picked up his tuxedo jacket, which he'd hung on the half-back of the bar stool. Intrigued, he quickly crossed the black and white tiles of the lobby floor, his exit blocked by a white haired couple who'd stopped just inside the lobby to watch the activity outside.

"Dammit," Seth muttered.

At six-foot-two he was able to look over the heads to see Leah Hamilton—married just six hours ago—arguing with a uniformed policeman. The cop wasn't paying her any attention; he just calmly opened the back door to the police van and offered her a hand to help her climb up into the dark interior.

Skimming past the old people, who had no intention of moving from their prime vantage point, Seth slapped his hand onto the outside door and pushed it open. It was supposed to be autumn in Cape Town but summer was still having too much fun and warm and fragrant air caressed his face as he stepped outside. It was a beautiful night…

…to be arrested.

Seth called out to Leah but the sound of a motorbike backfiring drowned his words. The police van was parked down the road from the entrance of the old hotel and his view of Leah was momentarily obscured when a small tourist bus pulled up next to him. Doors slid open and happy, and sun-broiled, tourists stumbled out, very cheerful after an evening of wine tasting.

Seth pushed his way through the throng and when he emerged, he saw the policeman slamming the back door shut and movement behind the grilled window suggested that Leah had lost the argument.

She was well and truly busted.

What the hell happened, Seth wondered as he broke into a jog. How did she go from looking utterly gorgeous, ridiculously happy, and legally married to being arrested?

The policeman turned at Seth's shout and watched his approach with cynical eyes. Seth noticed his hand hovering over his weapon so he lifted his own hands to show he wasn't a threat. Dark brown eyes met his in a challenging stare and he didn't drop his hand.

Dammit, suspicious and experienced. Seth might not be able to talk his way into getting them to release Leah.

"What did she do?' Seth asked, after greeting the cop with a polite good evening.

"And you are?" Cynical cop asked.

"A friend."

The cop's expression told him he'd had a long and annoying evening and he wasn't in the mood for small talk.

Seth, who believed in going to the heart of the matter, nodded to the locked door on the van. "Okay, arrest her. But let me go with her."

"You her husband?"

"No and I think you know that I'm not. Where is he and why are you arresting her?" Seth demanded, his voice sharpening and taking on a commanding officer note. He noticed the annoyed expression and the snap of the cop's spine. Dammit. Foreign cops did not appreciate Yanks ordering them around.

"She'll be charged at the Bellville Station, you can go there."

Hell, no. He wasn't leaving her alone, not for one damned minute. Seth opened his mouth to try another tactic and silently cursed when a female cop left the passenger seat of the van and joined her colleague. She looked even more exhausted than her partner and he could tell the delay was dancing on her last remaining nerve. He was keeping her from hot food or a hot shower or hot sex and she wasn't in the mood to listen to anything he had to say.

In thirty seconds he could disarm both and spring Leah but there were witnesses. The two old ducks were still standing just inside the door of the hotel, watching him and a few of the not-so-drunk revelers were also watching his futile argument. And he'd noticed three cameras covering the entrance of the hotel; everything he did was being recorded for prosperity.

Tiresome.

The easiest, and quickest, way to his objective was to give them a reason to arrest his ass. Without further thought, Seth clenched his fist and plowed it into the doughy flesh of the policeman's gut, pulling his punch at the last minute so he didn't cause much pain or do any damage. As he intended, they had his face plastered against the pavement a minute later—their reaction times were seriously slow—and then the business end of a nine millimeter was pushed under his chin.

Seth relaxed his body and allowed them to manhandle them, a little concerned about a shaky finger on the trigger of that semi-automatic. He slowed his breathing and resisted the urge to slap the weapon away, to retaliate. His default reaction was to fight his way out of a situation and it took a lot of willpower to allow the male cop to place a knee in his kidney, to grind his cheek into the filthy sidewalk.

Leah Hamilton, you owe me one.

He grimaced when they yanked his arms back, secured him with a pair of old cuffs, and yanked him to his feet. The fat cop screamed at him and the female cop waved her pistol around. Seth kept his eyes on her finger against the trigger, hoping like hell the safety was on.

When they finally calmed the hell down without, thank God, a weapon being discharged or a fist flying, they tossed him into the back of the police van. He stayed on the floor and scooted to the side panel and leaned back, stretching out his long legs. Damn, he had a tear on the cuff of his dress pants.

He looked up at Leah who was staring down at him, eyes and mouth perfectly round with surprise. "Seth? What the hell?"

Seth's mouth tipped upwards. "So, congratulations on your wedding, Leah."

"That being said," he added, "I'm no expert on weddings and marriage but even I can tell that yours isn't off to the best start."

LEAH HAMILTON LIFTED the heavy skirt of her elaborate wedding gown and hiked it up to reveal shapely calves and a pair of ridiculously high stilettos covered in what looked like crystals and pearls. Stomping over to the cement bench at the back of the jail, she sat and reached down and pulled her right shoe off and wiggled her siren red, sexy-as-hell tipped toes.

Seth leaned back and rested his head on the cool but grimy wall. His cellmate had, along with her pretty feet, a tiny waist, porcelain skin, and eyes the color of a stunning African day. Her long, dark hair fell out of her elaborate wedding-day hairstyle and her eye makeup was ruined, making her look like a horror movie bride. Yet Leah, with her red-rimmed eyes, her grubby wedding dress, and her bare feet, looked stunning. She was, by a galaxy or two, the sexiest cellmate he'd ever had.

Seth stretched out his long legs and shoved his hands into the pockets of his tuxedo pants and tuned out the drunken snores of the guest in the cell next door. Looking around, he decided this holding cell wasn't so bad. He'd been in a lot worse. And, for a change, his companion wasn't a gangbanger, a drunken wife beater, or a trainee serial killer but the utterly gorgeous and stupidly sexy younger sister of his best friend.

Oh, yeah, he'd definitely had worse experiences in jail.

"Why are you here?" Leah demanded and he heard the wobble in her voice.

Seth rolled his head to look at her. She was trying to sound brave but he could see the fear in her eyes.

"You're my best friend's sister. When I saw you being led out through the lobby of the hotel, in handcuffs, towards a police van, I thought that you could do with some company," Seth replied, on a careless shrug. "Jed would do the same thing for my sister."

He didn't bother to tell her that seeing that cop's thick fingers around her wrist made his teeth slam together so hard his jaw still ached.

"You saw me in the lobby? Why were you there after midnight?" Leah demanded.

"Drinking in the hotel bar."

"But there was free alcohol at the reception."

Seth looked at her, knowing his expression was inscrutable. He'd ducked out of the reception shortly after the speeches, ten minutes after Jed and McKenna left. Making small talk wasn't something he did well and he was over watching Leah fawn over the douche she'd married. Despite only meeting the groom earlier that evening and not exchanging more than ten words with him, Seth could tell he was an asshat by his fishy handshake and his refusal to make eye contact.

Seth also noticed Heath-the-Asshat looked anything but happy to be married. Leah glowed and looked as radiant as a bride should while Heath just looked like he'd sold his soul to the devil.

Leah put her shoe back on, wincing as she lowered her foot to the floor. She rested her forearms on her knees and Seth stared at her profile, wondering if the creamy skin of her elegant neck felt as soft as it looked.

"So you just jumped into that police van with me?"

"Yep."

Leah frowned at him, her expression disbelieving. "And they just let you?"

Well, no. There was no point in explaining how he got himself arrested, that it was the most efficient means to achieve his objective, which was to accompany Leah to jail so he could protect her for as long as she was inside, whether that was two hours or two days. He wasn't worried about the charges; Pytheon would make those go away.

There were perks to being the COO of a kick-ass international security company with high-level connections to many governments all around the world. Because of his position and because Leah was Jed's sister—Jed had recently retired after many years as a Pytheon operative—Stone, their el presidente, would exert pressure on high-level government officials to get Leah's charges dropped as well. Depending, of course, on why she was arrested.

Drunk and disorderly they could work with; murder would be a lot trickier. Not impossible but trickier.

Seth's eyes traveled over the beaded bodice of her torso, lingered on the hint of a cleavage, and wandered down and over the full skirt of her cream gown. Her perfect nails suggested she hadn't been in a fight and there was no trace of blood on her gown. Leah hadn't shot or stabbed her groom.

Seth relaxed; they'd be out before dawn.

"Aren't you going to ask me what happened?"

"Did you kill, badly hurt, or maim your asshat groom?"

Leah's extraordinary eyes widened in shock. "No!" she retorted.

"Pity."

Leah stared at him in shock and then the starch went out of her spine. She released a snort that was part laugh and part sob.

"I wish I had," she admitted, lifting up her hand to her head.

Seth watched, fascinated, as she started to pull tiny pins from her hair, the moisture in his mouth disappearing as sable colored curls fell to her shoulders and down her back. He made the mistake of dropping his eyes from her hair to her chest and noticed her breasts were higher, the fabric of her gown lower and, shit, he could just see a hint of a berry red nipple.

His erection sprang from half-mast to full and he casually sat up, leaning forward to disguise the party in his pants. He was thirty-five years old, and he was reacting like a teenager seeing his first centerfold. God, he needed to get laid.

Leah placed the final pin on the pile between them and pushed both her hands into her hair, shaking out the curls. "That's better," she murmured.

For who? Not for him, that was damn sure. He was painfully hard, fighting the urge to grab her, lay her on the concrete bench, and to pull up that heavy skirt and find out whether she was as wet and warm and spicy as he imagined her to be.

Wanting Leah wasn't anything new to Seth. She'd been the star of his action filled dreams—the only action he'd had lately—from the first minute he laid eyes on her six months ago.

Thinking about an unavailable woman was like waiting for a boat at an airport, constantly disappointing. He'd run through the endless list of why he should stop his thoughts wandering to her—she was about to be married, they lived on different continents, he was based in New York city, she lived here in Cape Town. He wasn't looking for a relationship; his idea of commitment was a one-night stand and Leah, according to Jed, didn't sleep around. Also, Leah was Jed's baby sister. Seth's junk didn't care.

He wanted Leah when she was engaged, wanted her as she walked down the aisle, wanted her now. He'd love to strip her out of that gown, peel the fancy, crystal-beaded bodice off her torso and touch his tongue to her nipple, to run his hands up the inside of her thighs...

"Are you going to ask me what happened?"

Seth blinked and it took a couple of seconds for him to

refocus, for her words to make sense. He ran a hand across his jaw, his hand scraping across his three day stubble.

"What happened?" he asked, thinking a little conversation might distract him from imagining her naked.

"I trashed the honeymoon suite." Leah stated. "Ripped the curtains, broke vases, tossed a champagne bottle at the TV set."

Since he dealt with scumbags of the earth, who routinely did a lot worse, a trashed hotel room didn't even blip on his bad deeds radar. "Okay. Why?"

Leah stared at the iron bars in front of her as a tear tracked mascara down her cheek. "Heath said he was going to go up, that I should stay and talk to my friends. I thought his suggestion was odd and told him that we could go up together."

"He insisted that I stay, said this wasn't our first time together, that it was just like any other party." Leah shook her head. "I was hurt by that comment and a little pissed off but I didn't want to start an argument on our wedding night. So, I stayed downstairs and after an hour I headed on up."

Judging by her wobbling chin Seth knew he wasn't going to like the next part of the story.

"I was supposed to call him, tell him when I was coming up, wake him up in case he'd fallen asleep. I didn't call, I just went up."

Seth didn't need a degree in quantum physics to know what she was about to say next. "And when you got up there, you caught him with someone else."

"Not just anyone else, I caught him with his best man, or

best woman...with the woman who'd stood up for him at the altar. The one in the red gown." Leah ran her fingers over her forehead. "They've been friends since they were kids. I thought they were just friends. Anyway, I found them on the bed and Sara was kissing the hell out of him. And Heath was kissing her back, with a lot more enthusiasm than he'd ever kissed me."

"Oh, shit," Seth said.

Her deep blue eyes filled with tears and her luscious bottom lip trembled. Unable to keep his distance, he scooted up the bench and put his arm around her slim shoulders, pulling her into his side. He dropped his lips onto her hair and closed his eyes.

Leah turned herface into his shoulder and her hand slid inside his jacket and her hand fisted the fabric of his shirt. "I never once suspected, I thought they were just good friends."

Leah shuddered. He pulled back, shrugged out of his jacket, and draped it around her shoulders. Leah looked up at him, her eyes darker with pain and despair. "Why did he want to marry me if I wasn't what he wanted?"

Money probably had something to do with it. Her father, General Hamilton, was wealthy and, as Jed had once told him, their mother's parents were loaded. Leah was, as he'd also heard, one of the most successful property developers in the city. Apparently, for someone just shy of thirty, Leah played with the big boys and frequently won the game. That took stones and cash.

Heath didn't have the first but obviously wanted the last.

Leah dropped her forehead onto his shoulder and her

tears dampened the fabric of his dress shirt. Seth lifted his hand up to hold the back of her head, wishing he could massage her pain away.

"I always wondered why he wasn't keen on sex, why he never seemed to want me. I'd wear naughty lingerie, greet him at the door naked, I sent him super sexy texts." Leah snapped her head back and her eyebrows pulled together. "It's not like we didn't have sex, we did. And it was great, well, good. Sort of. Maybe he's just confused and Sara caught him at a weak moment."

Oh, hell, no.

Seth grabbed her chin and tipped it up so he was looking into her eyes. "Heath is a dickhead. You caught him making out with someone else, on your *wedding night*! His behavior is inexcusable so don't you dare try and rationalize it." Seth made an effort to sound soothing. "Trust me, this isn't about you but about the fact that Heath wanted to live off you, wanted his cream-cake and to eat it, too."

"But maybe if I was sexier, hotter..."

"Honey, if you were any hotter you'd melt the sun." Seth growled and placed his thumb on her bottom lip. His lips quirked. "You're the sexiest, hottest, most beautiful bride I've ever seen."

Leah's tears disappeared and he saw something spark in her eyes. Desire, maybe? Whatever it was, it was followed by doubt. And confusion, bucketloads of confusion.

Wanting to give her something else to think about but also because he'd always wanted to taste her, Seth dropped his head and swiped his mouth over her lips. He felt her shock and waited for her to pull back, to slap his face, to tear a verbal strip off him.

When she did neither, Seth pulled his mouth off hers and bent his head so their eyes were level. "Your husband is an effing idiot and I'm going to show you exactly how sexy you are."

Seth didn't give her time to respond; he slammed his mouth on hers and hoped his kiss conveyed that she was all woman, sexy as hell, utterly perfect. His hands traced the cord down the side of her neck and slipped under the fabric of his jacket to trace her collarbone, down her chest. His tongue tangled with hers, long, slow, sexy swipes that had his head reeling. She was heat and fire and passion and he felt the walls of the jail cell disappear. He could only think of Leah; he loved her spicy, decadent mouth and marveled over the fact that her perfect skin was so smooth, so silky, so girly. Seth nibbled his way across her jaw, pulled her delicate earlobe into his mouth and smiled when she shuddered.

"You are all woman, soft and gorgeous and so very sexy." Seth growled in her ear. He dragged a finger down her breast and felt her nipple pucker. He wished he could pull her bodice down and taste her, but swiftly reminded himself that kissing her in a squalid jail cell was one thing, he couldn't take this any further.

If they weren't sitting behind bars, he could seduce her into making love, but he knew that he would be taking advantage of her broken heart, her need for attention. Besides, should he ever be that lucky to take Leah to bed he wanted her to want him, to be thinking of him and only him. He wasn't any woman's panacea for pain.

Seth lifted his hand to cradle her cheek and his fingers pushed past her hairline, and soft, fragrant curls fell over his knuckles.

"Leah, look at me." Seth commanded and when her eyes met his, he spoke again. "This isn't about you, about how hot or sexy or attractive you are. This isn't about how loving you are or how good you are in bed. This is about the fact he is a tool who needs his face rearranged." Seth's thumb gently stroked her cheekbone. "You are gorgeous, incredibly, breathtakingly hot. If you don't remember anything else I said tonight, remember that."

Leah pulled her bottom lip between her teeth as she nodded.

"He treated you like crap, Leah. When this passes and he wants to talk, don't forget that," Seth said, his tone low but insistent.

"Okay," Leah agreed.

"You won't allow him to talk his way out of it?"

"No."

"Halcott! Hamilton-Green!"

Seth snapped his head up at the yell and the sound of boots hitting cement suggested someone was walking towards their cell. Seth moved away from Leah and winked at her as he slouched against the wall, his face insouciant.

A big policeman approached the bars, his blue shirt stretched across his enormous belly. "Charges against both of you have been dropped. You're free to go," He said, unlocking the cell door and pushing it open.

Seth stood up and, as he held out his hand to Leah to help her up, he saw Jed and McKenna approach the cell, both worried. McKenna rushed into the cell and pulled Leah into her arms. Leah, as expected, burst into tears. Thunderclouds appeared in Jed's eyes.

"Your brother-in-law desperately needs a come-to-Jesus talk." Seth told him.

Jed looked at his wife and sister and nodded. When he looked at Seth, he was wearing his I-want-to-kill-someone expression. "I'm on it."

Seth clapped him on the shoulder as he walked past him. "Yeah, so am I."

"WHAT THE HELL do you mean we can't trace that email?"

Seth slammed his hands onto his hips and looked up at the high ceiling of his incident room, searching for the calm and the patience he was reputed to have. He looked down at the still swollen fingers on his hand and grimaced; it seemed as though he'd left those two traits as well as his mind back in Cape Town when he left two weeks before. His eyes were watching Cracker's hands dance across the keyboard but on his mental big screen another set of images flashed—Leah, touching her top lip with the pink tip of her tongue after he kissed her, her wedding hair mussed from his hands. The desire in her blue eyes, the confusion. The fear on Heath Green's face when he placed his forearm across his throat and lifted him onto his toes, the ache in his hand after he plowed his fist into the dry wall an inch to the left of asshat's eye, seeing Leah sitting on a lounger on her verandah, her arms around her knees, tears running down her face. It had taken everything he had to say goodbye, to walk away from her.

Seth scrubbed his hands over his face and told himself to concentrate. He was back in New York, was back at work, and he needed to focus. Leah would be okay… she just needed time.

Cracker's blond dreadlocks bounced as he monitored the reams of code running across his screen. Cracker was his most creative hacker, and if he was having trouble pinning down the IP address of the computer The Recruiter's latest taunting email was sent from, then the rest of his hackers—all ten of them—didn't have a chance.

Crap!

When Cracker shook his head and leaned back in his chair, Seth muttered a string of long and creative curses.

"Sorry, boss," Cracker muttered.

Seth laid a hand on his shoulder to reassure the young man—God, was he even twenty yet?—that he wasn't upset with him. He was just deeply pissed off that a scumbag was running around the world, selling his services as a recruiter for any cult who could pay him his enormous fee. As someone who'd grown up in a cult-like commune, who'd escaped the rigid, crazy world—the notion of someone actively recruiting members, usually teenagers, to join organizations for a financial reward was even more despicable than the cults themselves.

And any group or individual who twisted the tenets of

various religions to suit their own egotistical agenda were fucking despicable indeed.

Seth felt a presence beside him and looked sideways at Smith Stone, a philanthropist billionaire and the president of Pytheon International, a non-cult-like organization whose sole purpose was to right the wrongs that governments, the military, and police organizations couldn't. Sometimes that meant fudging the rules, coloring outside the lines, using a lot of coercion, threats and, yeah, sometimes that meant annihilation. Of a structure, of a bank account and, very infrequently, a person.

Like him, Stone was prepared to make the hard decisions, to issue the order. They both understood that playing by the rules didn't work in certain circumstances and they needed to be creative to get the job done.

And they always, always got the job done.

The Recruiter was at the top of Seth's shoot first, talk later list.

"What are we working on?" Stone demanded, his deep voice holding a hint of command.

Just a hint because, as Seth had told him before, he gave the orders in his incident room. They were both determined, driven alpha males, leaders of the pack and they frequently bumped heads but Seth trusted Stone. He respected Stone and he knew that the trust and respect was returned.

Stone was, in fact, the closest he had to a friend now that Jed had married McKenna, retired from Pytheon and taken to sailing the high seas with McKenna and her daughter, Daisy.

"Ismail Khan, super-wealthy and influential South Africa businessman, contacted us this morning. He's a moderate Muslim, and heads a foundation that is world-renowned for humanitarian efforts around the world. Very well respected..." Seth nodded to Cracker and pictures appeared on the large monitor that covered most of the wall. "Wife, Fatima, sons Muhammad—currently studying in London—and Fayed. Daughter Sadiyah."

Stone crossed his arms and watched the pictures fly across the wall. "What's the problem?"

"Fayed has disappeared. Packed up, swiped some cash from his mother, caught the bus for school but never arrived," Seth answered.

"And why have we been contacted?" Stone asked, shoving his hands into the pockets of his suit pants.

"He's wealthy, he's connected, and he thinks his son has been radicalized. He wants us to find him."

They'd tracked a few kids who'd joined radical Islamic sects across the Middle East. Some they'd managed to return to their parents before they were fully indoctrinated, never to be heard from again. Some they lost. It was too soon to speculate on what Fayed's fate would be. All Seth knew was that he'd do his best to get Fayed home.

"And what organization do we think he's joined?" Stone asked.

Seth shrugged. "Hard to tell as yet. The kid is an amateur hacker; pretty good if the father is to be believed. It might be that cell we've heard rumors about, an internet-based organization that uses vulnerable and disenfranchised teenagers to hack systems, organizations. It's cyber terrorism. They are exceptionally well-funded, very computer savvy, and are open to using any means to recruit new members to join the cause."

"Tell me what you're thinking," Stone said, narrowing his dark eyes. "And why do you have an image of The Recruiter up on the screen? Do you think he's involved?"

Seth leaned over Cracker and brought up the message they'd been trying to trace. "We received this ten minutes ago."

"The Recruiter many, Halcott none." Stone read the words. His eyes narrowed on the screen. "The asswipe is taunting you now? By sending you a photo of Fayed?"

"Yeah, I've become part of the game." Seth frowned at the image of the teen on the large screen. The kid was tall and gangly and had the beginnings of a mustache. His dark eyes blazed with intelligence. "He's taunting me, wanting us to think that he's omnipotent, that he can take kids from anywhere in the world, that he's untouchable."

"Big ego."

"Oh, yeah," Seth agreed. "Hopefully his hubris will cause him to make a mistake."

Seth stared at the screen, mulling over the facts. He was going to nail this fucker if it was the last thing he did. "You want to play, dickhead? I'm your guy," he stated before turning his attention back to Stone. "I'm going to go to Cape Town, and I'm going to nail his balls to the nearest wall."

Stone rubbed his chin. "I really need to explain to you,

again, the concept of what working for a boss entails, Halcott."

"I'm *going*, Stone."

"We're short of agents, I need you here," Stone argued.

"Tough." Seth ran his hand over the back of his neck. "Hire more people, Stone."

"I'm going through the applications right now; hopefully I'll have a couple of candidates to add to the payroll soon," Stone replied.

Seth nodded and his cell phone vibrated in his pocket. "I'm not discussing this, Stone." Seth reiterated, pulling out his phone. Seeing that it was Jed, via a satellite phone, he turned the screen to show Stone who was calling before putting the phone to his ear.

Jed sounded a million miles away, which he, sort of, was. Seth nodded to Cracker, who immediately tracked the signal of Jed's phone. They were fifty nautical miles south of the Cook Islands and within seconds Cracker had the latest picture of his yacht taken by one of the many satellites orbiting earth. Seth had never asked Cracker how he hacked into satellites and wasn't sure if he needed to know. He was just grateful for Cracker's skills and he grinned at the picture of the yacht taken yesterday morning that Cracker put up on the big screen. Daisy, five years old, was fishing off the stern and Mac was sitting next to her. McKenna was reading a book and all seemed well with their world.

Poor guy; sexy wife, cute kid, tropical seas, and sunshine.

"What's up?" Seth asked.

The connection via the sat phone was scratchy and Seth

could only hear the third of every word Jed spoke.

"Leah said...scratch scratch...tell you...said she met... scratch, scratch...sounds fishy."

"I can't hear you, dude."

"Call Leah...explain...Signal weak... Keep...eye on us."

Yeah, Jed knew Seth could track him and was happy for him to do it. Jed, like him, knew that a pretty location and warm weather didn't mean trouble was also on vacation. He'd been an operative long enough and knew Pytheon routinely used satellite images, illegally acquired, on many ops.

"Tell Mac not to sunbathe nude on the deck." Seth teased him.

"Not... first rodeo...Call Leah, important."

The call dropped and Seth frowned. From Jed's garbled message he heard the three of them—Jed, McKenna and Daisy—were fine but there seemed to be something up Jed's sister, Leah. Jed's very sexy sister, Leah. She of the sexy toes and the ultra-brief marriage.

Seth ignored Stone's inquiring face and held up his hand to ward off his questions. He swiped his thumb over the screen of his encrypted smart phone and scrolled through his contacts. When he pushed the green icon to dial Leah Hamilton his heart, to his annoyance, bounced off his ribs.

Leah answered within two rings, her voice polite and businesslike. "Leah Hamilton, how can I help you?"

Since his number could not be traced, Seth introduced himself and he heard her suck in a deep breath. "Jed, McKenna—"

"They're fine, Leah." Seth hastened to assure her. "I spoke to Jed a minute ago but the connection was really bad. I think he was trying to tell me that I should call you."

"That's a relief," Leah replied. "Well, I spoke to him a couple of days ago, McKenna is doing well, she felt had a bit of morning sickness but seems to be over it now."

Oh, yeah, his best friends were pregnant. He was happy for them but it wasn't something he could see in his future. Kids? Hell, no, he knew what could happen to them. Love, of a wife, of a family, wasn't on his agenda. He'd learned a very long time ago that the more he loved—valued—the more there was to lose. When what he valued was removed, the pain could be devastating and he'd planned to avoid it if he could.

"They are leaving the Cook Islands and are sailing towards New Zealand."

Seth heard the false note of cheeriness in Leah's voice and wondered how she was doing. He thought he should ask but he couldn't find the words. *Are you okay? Have you seen a lawyer? Do you think about that super-hot kiss we shared two weeks ago?*

Seth shook his head, needing all his willpower not to show just how much that memory, and her sexy voice, affected him. "So, what did Jed want you to tell me?"

"Oh, that… I met your dad. He was visiting Cape Town and he came by my office, told me that you and Jed had told him to look me up if he ever got to the city."

Not sure if he'd heard her properly, Seth forced the words through his constricted throat. "Sorry, who did you say came to your offices?"

"Your dad, Ben Halcott."

That was what he'd thought she'd said, but that wasn't possible.

Seth told Leah to hold on and dropped his phone to hold it against his pants leg. He was sure someone was playing a sick joke on him and that Leah had her wires crossed but he always covered all his bases. His first instinct was to make sure his mom was safe. He tapped Cracker's shoulder. "Check the GPS in my mom's phone. Use whatever excuse you come up with to double-check what the GPS says. I want to know where she is, exactly."

Cracker nodded and whipped around to face his screen. Stone just folded his arms across his chest and lifted his eyebrows at Seth as he raised the phone back up to his ear. "I'm back," Seth said, his voice even. This was a bad joke, it had to be. "Can you describe him?"

"Add thirty years onto your face and that's what he looked like," Leah replied. "I took a selfie of us...I meant to send it to Jed to send to you but...with everything else... I forgot."

"You have a picture of him?" Dear God, she had an image?

Excellent! Yet his cynical side issued a quick warning—a picture and an easy identification was too damn easy and he smelled a dozen rats. What was this guy's game? What was this message, what was he trying to say? Why Cape Town, why Leah?

"I can send it to you if you want," Leah said. "But you

need to give me your number. It didn't come up on my screen."

"Send it to my email address."

"Leah, I'll get back to you," Seth muttered when she was done taking his details and winced when he heard how abrupt he sounded. It couldn't be helped. He was abrupt and this was important. Besides, explanations weren't his thing.

"Your mom is at work," Crackersaid, replacing the handset of his phone.

"You spoke to her?"

"Yeah, I –"

"Doesn't matter." Seth whipped back. "Access my inbox, Cracker."

Cracker flicked a glance between to Stone and back to Seth. "I don't think I can—"

"Cut the crap." Seth barked. "If you can hack into defense satellites, you can hack into our inboxes. Do it."

Cracker winced but in ten seconds Seth's Inbox was displayed on the screen. "Open the latest email, the one from Leah Hamilton. Open the attachment."

A photograph appeared on the screen and Seth took ten seconds to look at Leah. Long, curly hair held back by her designer shades, blue eyes dim with sadness. *She'd been cheated on during her wedding night two weeks ago, what did you expect?* She wore a bright red sundress and her lipstick matched her dress—an obvious attempt to look cheerful even if she didn't feel it—and she took his breath away.

No time to think about the girl. Seth forced himself to look at the photo of the man standing next to Leah. He towered over her, big and broad compared to her petite frame. Leah was right. He did look a little like him. Nut brown hair flecked with gray, green eyes. A thin mouth slow to smile, the same rangy, naturally broad-shouldered, slim-hipped build.

Shit.

Stone sucked in a breath and looked at Seth, concern on his face. "That can't be him."

"Sure as hell looks like it could be, though." Seth responded, his expression grim.

Cracker spun his chair around and looked from Stone to Seth. "That guy could be your dad, boss."

"Yep."

Cracker frowned at Seth's machine gun response. "And is that a problem?"

"Yep," Seth replied as he exchanged a long, what-the-hell look with Stone.

He tipped his head and he and Stone walked away from the desks, away from interested ears. He trusted his staff, to an extent, but he never gave them more information than they needed to know. Frustrating sure, but this was his incident room and his rules and keeping secrets protected lives.

"Don't jump to conclusions. There are similarities but there are also enough differences for me to be doubtful. Besides, only DNA can prove it." Stone stated.

"If he's an imposter, what's his agenda?" Seth asked.

"And if he's your father, why hasn't he contacted you before this? Father or not, imposter or not, this guy knows a lot about you. He knows Jed, knows that Jed has a sister, knows that this picture, this news would eventually get back to you," Stone said and pulled out his phone. He quickly typed and after a couple of minutes, he looked back up at Seth. "I'll contact the police in Spring, that's where your father lived, wasn't it? I'll ask them what definitive proof they had that the body in the burned out car was Ben Halcott's."

"Age, build, wallet, personal items. He was known to drive that car."

"Still circumstantial," Stone replied. "I want DNA or dental records."

"I do, too," Seth admitted.

Seth tapped the back of his phone with a long finger. "I'm going to Cape Town, I'll see if I can track him down."

"Going to be hard, it's a big city." Stone pointed out.

"But there's a reason he's there. He made contact with Leah, made a concerted effort to grab my attention." Seth rolled his shoulders attempting to relieve the tension gathered there. "I need to know why."

Seth walked back to Cracker and Stone followed. "Bring up Fayed Khan." He ordered.

Cracker hit a button on his keyboard and the screen returned to the previous subject of the radicalized boy. He was missing and he needed to be found. If Seth went to Cape Town he could kill two birds with one stone. And he could lay eyes of Leah again. Check that she was okay and that asshat Heath wasn't trying to worm his way back into her life.

Laying eyes on Leah was always a pleasure. Laying hands on her would be even better. Seth shook his head, annoyed at where his thoughts went. Leah…even thinking about her was a distraction. Why her? What was so special about Jed's sister that he couldn't forget about her? He didn't allow anything, especially woman, to distract him from his missions.

Besides, Leah was going through a tough breakup, was dealing with a broken heart. *Remember that, Halcott.*

"I'll go to Cape Town, look into the missing kid, if you take over here." Seth told Stone.

Stone sent him a hard look. "Can you be objective about either of these two missions? Looking for your father and The Recruiter? Loss of objectivity can lead to mistakes and mistakes get you a headstone."

Stone had a right to be concerned. His parents had been members of a small cult—a crazy-ass grouping of free spirits—and, to be honest, he still wasn't sure what they actually believed in, if they believed in anything at all. The cult lived in a commune on the outskirts of Spring, a one horse town in the coal country of eastern Kentucky. When he was four, he and his mother left the commune and his father had not taken that news well. He found them in the next town over and made his displeasure known by rearranging his mom's face and dragging her home. His brave and enterprising mother waited for her broken body to heal and they escaped again. Believing he would kill her if he found them again, he and his mother became nomadic, constantly changing identities to fly under the radar. As a result, he grew up overprotected, constantly looking over his shoulder and scared.

Sick of living scared, he'd joined the military straight after school and, after a stint in the Ranger's, made his way into Delta Force, the best of the best. Nothing scared him anymore...but his pathological hatred of any organization that promoted extremism in any form remained.

So, hell, okay...he wasn't objective but that wouldn't stop him from doing his job. He'd find Fayed and he'd find The Recruiter. And he'd find his fake father...

His highly specialized and extensive military training had taught him to separate the job from his emotions. He had the ability to operate with detachment, to do the job no matter what the cost.

He didn't fail. Ever.

Seth raised his eyebrows at Stone, who cracked a small smile. "Okay, I'll step in here. You need to update me on what operations we are currently running."

Seth nodded. "Most of the operations are under control, there's no need for you to interfere. The agents like to do their own thing so we need to trust their skills and intelligence."

"Just like I trust you to run this show," Stone said, amused. "I might not be army, Halcott, but this isn't my first rodeo."

Not my first rodeo, said in exactly the same tone Jed used. Hmmm.

Seth looked at Stone as they made their way to the private offices at the back of the incident rooms. When Stone made comments like that, he implied he was more than a rich boy with a fancy education, that he'd seen more action than he was prepared to admit. When Seth had first joined Pytheon, he had done a little digging of his own but nothing he'd learned about Stone suggested Stone was anything more than a smart, rich executive with an Ivy League education. But he'd seen the guy work out in the gym, on the range. Stone was a skilled marksman and even better at hand to hand combat. He had the skills that men didn't learn in rich-boy gyms.

Stone had a superb cover story and it pissed Seth off that he couldn't break it. Despite the fact he loathed not having all the puzzle pieces, he knew, instinctively, Stone was rock solid and that he had Seth's back.

And, really, that was all that mattered.

SINCE SPEAKING TO Seth yesterday, Leah found herself looking at the photograph of Seth's dad more than she should and thinking of her and Seth's odd conversation. Seth sounded as he usually did, super cool, super detached, and absolutely nothing like the passionate, sexy, intense man who'd kissed her with such expertise. Leah frowned and pushed a strand of hair behind her right ear. Lately she'd spent a lot of time thinking about Seth and his kiss. It was a brilliant distraction from thinking about her sham-wedding, catching her husband kissing Sara, dealing with the lawyers in an attempt to get their marriage annulled, the hurt, and the humiliation. Leah latched onto everything that allowed her a moment's respite from thinking about her messed up life and that was why she'd accepted Ben's offer to buy her lunch.

Unlike his reserved, cool, sexy son, Ben had been a harmless, charming, old flirt and she'd immediately responded to and appreciated the mischievous twinkle in his eyes. He'd been entertaining company but his habit of deflecting the subject away from Seth and his childhood had been very disappointing. Jed and Seth, super soldiers, were, to say the least, economical with words. She knew very little about Jed's best friend and she'd hoped to learn more from Ben, but he'd ducked her questions about his son so Leah walked away from that lunch knowing nothing more about Seth. And, boy, she was desperate to learn more about the man who'd kissed her with such skill.

Because he was an excellent distraction from thinking about Heath. Leah blew air into her cheeks and looked at the ceiling. She fully accepted she spent far too much time thinking about Seth, thinking about his kiss...his hands, his scent. And when she was being very honest, brutally honest, she admitted she wished he'd taken that kiss further, that he'd given her more than ahot kiss. There had to be something wrong with her when her hottest sexual memory in years was a brief kiss in a filthy jail cell a few hours after she said "I do" to another man.

But when she pushed Seth aside, thoughts of Heath barreled in. *Why did he marry me? Was everything a big lie to get my money? Did he love me, at all?*

Am I ever going to live down the humiliation? What must our guests think, our friends, my family? Why the hell didn't I listen to Jed when he told me that marrying Heath was a stupid-ass idea? And, most worrying, why aren't I more upset? Why is my heart just bruised, not broken?

A fist knocking against the rim of her office door made Leah look up and her stomach instantly did back flips and her lungs forgot how to inflate. Worn jeans, a fire-engine red t-shirt stretched across a broad chest fell loosely over a flat and very hard stomach, legs that went on for miles. Seth pushed his designer sunglasses into his thick hair and his large hand rubbed his stubble-covered jaw.

Fallen angel face. Gorgeous, but oh so troubled.

Leah took a deep breath and leaned back in her chair. She resisted the urge to place her hands under her thighs so Seth wouldn't see them shaking.

She needed her cool voice, her I-can-deal-with-anyone voice.

"Seth Halcott." She drawled, crossing her legs, noticing Seth's eyes lingered on the hem of her short skirt.

The temperature in the room rocketed up and she felt the moisture in her mouth disappear. He was so damn…male. Hot. Hard. Sexy.

Aw, no. Not good. *It's just a chemical reaction, lust attraction. Life's way of telling her that she wasn't dead, that she will feel normal again.*

"So, you were the last person I expected to waltz into my office at eleven-forty on a Thursday morning." Leah stated, watching as he stepped into the room, dropped a backpack to the floor, and kicked the door closed behind him.

Unlike his father, he didn't bother to ask whether this was a good time for her, whether she was busy, whether he could take her to lunch…to bed.

Not helpful, Hamilton. And you're only thinking that way because he'd be a wonderful way to escape your ultra-shitty life at the moment.

"Leah, you are looking…" Seth said in his deep, growly, I-smoke-a-hundred-cigarettes-before-breakfast voice. Sexy, attractive, doable?

"Good," he continued. "You're looking good. Better than I expected."

He was being kind.

"But you're still pale, look thinner and you have bags under your eyes."

"Gee, thanks for the effusive compliments," Leah retorted.

But Seth looked, doable, sexy, hot—and more—but he also looked exhausted. His eyes were red rimmed and his hair looked like he'd been running his hands through it on a continuous basis. She'd barely finished the thought when his big, tanned ringless hand pushed through those thick, wavy strands.

"I presume you being here has something to do with your father?"

When Seth just looked at her, his face inscrutable and eyes unreadable, Leah lifted her hands and explained. "I haven't spoken to you since that night…"

The night we kissed. He might not have verbalized the

words but she knew he was thinking about that kiss. Oh, nothing on his face gave him away but his eyes darkened to a smoky green.

Not going there, not going there…

"I tell you about having lunch with your dad, I send you the picture of the two of us, and thirty-six hours later you're here. Why?"

Seth looked at her and Leah tried not to squirm. "He's not my dad."

"I'm sorry, but you look exactly the same. There is no way you are not related to that man. You even have the same sex…scratchy voice."

Please let him not have caught my slip.He does not need to know he is my favorite, late night, triple x-rated fantasy. Amusement appeared in Seth's eyes and disappeared ten seconds later. "He can't be my father. I'm thinking this is some strange mistake."

"Why?"

"Because my father is dead."

Chapter Two

SETH LEANED BACK in his chair. His eyes felt like they'd been scrubbed with sandpaper and caffeine saturated blood pumped sluggishly through his system. He he'd been tossed into a game not knowing the rules, but that was okay, he'd make up his own. But he'd still like to know who the game master was and what his motives were.

And how did Leah fit in? Few people outside of Pytheon knew about his and Jed's connection; Seth's work was his life so he didn't socialize much and when he did, work was never a subject he discussed. Apart from the fact that Pytheon frequently bent rules to get the job done, the missions and objectives of the organization were a closely guarded secret and not something that came up in conversation at the cocktail parties he never attended.

Who knew about Jed and Leah? Cracker? Stone? His mom...

But why Leah? Why Cape Town?

He's separating me from my support base. Seth looked at a point beyond Leah's pretty head. *He thinks I would be weaker, more vulnerable, away from the States.*

Bullshit. Whoever was toying with him didn't know him very well if he thought that. Seth felt the reassuring weight of a Glock nestled against his spine. They had contacts all over the world and ten minutes after he cleared customs, he'd been handed a pack containing two unregistered firearms and a bag full of other big-boy toys. More vulnerable, his ass.

Leah coughed and Seth moved his eyes back to her face. For someone who'd been married, cheated on, and arrested in one evening she looked like she was doing okay. Tired, sure, a little sad but remarkably composed. Leah Hamilton was tough and he admired her resilience.

"Seth, you can't just drop a bombshell like and that and spend the next few minutes staring at the wall. What do you mean, your father is dead?"

Like any other woman, she liked explanations and that was problematic. He rarely explained and because he was consistently single, never explained himself to a woman. "Ten years ago we received word that my father died in a car accident—"

"You were living apart?"

"Since I was about four." There was no way he was going to explain his torrid history, that they'd spent most of their lives running from his father.

Whenever they started to get comfortable, get into a routine, his mom would get spooked and they'd be on the move again. His mom became a master of manipulating the system or changing identities, of earning and paying cash and flying under the radar. Maybe that was why he was such a good soldier, he'd been taught the art of evasion at a young age.

"And you don't recognize the man in the photo? He looks a lot like you."

"Everyone has a doppelganger," Seth replied, digging his thumb and index finger into his eyeballs. "Can you recall what you talked about? Did he say where he was from, what he was doing in Cape Town?"

Leah's arched eyebrows pulled together and Seth caught his breath. God, even her eyebrows were sexy. He was in deep, deep trouble. How was he supposed to figure out this latest situation when all the blood drained from his head to his crotch?

"He said he was here on holiday, he'd done a safari and was exploring Cape Town as every tourist does."

"Did he mention me? Jed?"

Leah pulled her bottom lip between her teeth before answering. "I was thinking about that, thinking that he was very reticent, very short on personal details. I just assumed it was family trait."

Seth didn't bother to respond to her comment. Yeah, sure, he was distant and emotionally unavailable, reticent. He'd spent most of his life being on his guard. Mistrusting people and their motives was a habit.

"He said he was your dad, Seth. He looked like you and he was a funny, charming guy. I took it at face value." Leah stated. "I didn't do anything wrong."

Seth made a concerted effort to relax his shoulders. It wasn't easy since he was tired and aggravated and turned on. "I'm not accusing you of doing something wrong. I'm just trying to make sense of this craziness." It was hard to keep the frustration out of his voice. "A couple more questions, okay?"

Leah nodded her agreement.

"Did he give you a contact number? Tell you where he was staying?"

"No."

Yeah, that would've been too easy. "Whose idea was it to take the photograph? Yours or his?"

Leah wrinkled her nose. "His... We took one on my phone, one on his. He asked me to send it on to you. He said he'd run out of air time and since he was leaving soon he didn't want to buy more air time and data."

"There are a million free Wi-Fi hot spots where he could've connected and sent it to me," Seth said, thinking aloud. "He doesn't have my number, can't get my number so he used you to get to me. It was his only access."

Leah rubbed her temples with the tips of her fingers. "This is crazy. And confusing. But somehow he knew of your connection to Jed and that I am Jed's sister."

"Yep." Seth leaned forward, grabbed her phone off her desk, and added his number to her contacts.

"Help yourself," Leah muttered.

Seth flashed her a quick grin, put the phone on the desk, and pushed it in her direction. "I just did. Call me if he gets in contact again, if anything happens—and I mean anything—that you think is odd." He stood up, jammed his hands in his pockets and tipped his head. "Do you know the suburb of Constantia well?"

Leah blinked at the change of subject. "Fairly well. I've sold a couple of properties there."

"Do you know Ismail Khan?"

"The philanthropist? That Ismail Khan?"

Seth nodded.

"I don't know him personally but I've heard of him. Why?"

Seth ignored her question and looked at his backpack at the door. "You still living in your grandparent's home?"

"Yes."

"Can I stay with you?" He didn't know he was going to ask the question until the words were out of his mouth.

But, right now, all he had going for him was his instinct, and it was insisting something was off and Leah was involved. He sensed this situation could turn from weird and odd to dangerous in a heartbeat and he couldn't protect her if he was living in a hotel across the city.

She wouldn't say no, he was her brother's best friend and hospitality ran through the Hamilton family like beer ran through bars.

He saw her hesitation but it was the flash of desire in her eyes that caught his attention. Oh, hell, the chemistry hadn't disappeared. If anything it now glowed hotter and brighter.

He had enough to deal with. He didn't need a hot, sexy woman distracting him as well. And she was just out of a nasty breakup…

"Sure," Leah said but she didn't sound sure at all.

Back out, go to a hotel, you're playing with fire…

"Thanks. What if I meet you back here at five and I follow you home?"

Leah nodded. She glanced at her computer monitor and back up at him. "I need to do an inspection on a house after work. You can either go home, I'll give you a key, or you can tag along."

He wanted to go directly home and hit the sack, pass out for a couple of hours but his gut instinct was still screaming it wasn't a good idea to leave her alone.

Enough of those acid-inducing thoughts. Seth picked up his pack and easily slung it over his shoulder. At the doorway he turned and looked back at her. "How are you doing? With the asshat situation?"

Lean pushed her hair back from her face and lifted one shoulder. "The lawyers have petitioned the court to have the marriage annulled."

Good. That was a start. "And emotionally? How are you coping?"

Leah pulled her bottom lip between her teeth and when she released it to speak, he noticed the teeth marks dotting her skin. "Good days and bad days. Sometimes relieved, sometimes sad, sometimes so angry I could kill someone."

"Sounds normal." But what the hell did he know? He'd never come remotely close to being committed, let alone married. "See you later."

Seth had one foot out the door when Leah called his name. He turned to look at her.

"I wanted to say thank you, for staying with me in jail, for being there. I might've fallen apart if you weren't there."

No, she wouldn't have. Leah was tougher than she realized. "You would've been okay but I'm glad I could help." He squinted at her. "Should I apologize for kissing you?"

Amusement, hot and cheerful, jumped into her eyes. "I'll

see you later, Halcott."

It didn't escape Seth's attention that she declined to answer his question. Seth walked out of her office and into the African sunshine, thinking a little part of him, a very tiny, minuscule part of him, was almost grateful to this current crazy situation for giving him an excuse to drop back into Leah's life.

★ ★ ★

SETH FOLLOWED LEAH into the hall of her house in Simon's Town and instantly felt at ease. The hall opened into an open plan lounge, dominated by a massive fireplace. Above the fireplace was an oversized seascape and while Seth didn't know his Turner from a turnip, he recognized the quality of the art. Beneath the painting were numerous photo frames but Seth was particularly interested in a photograph of a smiling woman who could only be Leah's mom. They shared the high cheekbones, the triangular face, the laughing eyes.

Two leather couches complemented the rich antique furniture and begged for a guest to grab a book and settle down. The flowers were fresh and plentiful and mingled with the smell of beeswax polish. As he followed Leah, Seth's eyes darted from the furniture to the art and the Persian rugs on the floor. He'd expected modern and minimalistic from Leah, not this easy combination of plump couches, fresh flowers, and old and new.

"I need a drink." Leah stated. She'd kicked her shoes off at the door and she was tugging her shirt out of the waistband of her skirt. "Do you need a drink?"

"Honestly, what I'd really like is a beer in the shower. That possible?" Seth asked, dropping his backpack from his shoulder to the floor. He ignored his exhaustion, knowing he could go for a lot longer without any sleep.

"Sure. Let me grab a beer and I'll show you to your room."

Seth leaned against the doorframe to the kitchen and watched as Leah yanked open the large fridge and Seth caught a glimpse of fruit and vegetables before she slammed the door shut. He was tired, sure, but he also felt like his stomach was eating itself. He hadn't eaten since the tiny breakfast he'd scoffed before he landed.

Leah handed him the beer. "While you're in the shower, I'll make us something to eat."

"You cook?"

"Sure. Don't you?"

Seth shook his head. "Not if I can help it. What are you going to make?"

Leah turned, opened the fridge door again and looked inside. "Chicken stir fry?"

"Sounds good." Actually, it sounded amazing; he hadn't had a home-cooked meal in weeks, possibly months. "I like your house."

Leah slammed the fridge door shut again and looked around. "I like it, too. I inherited this house and a smaller portion of the family trust fund via my maternal grandparents. Jed got a bigger share of the fund, which I am very okay with."

"You both have a hell of a work ethic and neither of you are trust-fund babies." Seth commented, picking the label off his beer.

"My father, the general, would never let us be." Leah tipped her head sideways and looked puzzled. "How do you know how hard I work?"

He'd never admit he listened, closely, when either Jed or McKenna spoke about Leah, more closely than he should. Hell, whenever anyone mentioned Leah's name his ears, and less convenient parts of his body, perked up.

"You and Mac are close, she talks about you often."

"I hit the wonderful-sister-in-law jackpot," Leah admitted, leaning against the kitchen counter. "I love Jed dearly but she's everything he's not; warm, open, relaxed." Leah wrinkled her nose. "That wasn't supposed to be a criticism, I understand that Mac and I have the luxury of running our mouths, we're not soldiers, spies, retrieval experts, and we don't run missions where people's lives are at stake. Unlike you, we don't have the responsibility of running the operations at Pytheon," Leah said, her tone low but her eyes steady on his face.

Seth pushed his thumb under the strap of his backpack and kept his face unreadable. "What do you know of Pytheon?"

"That it is, at its core, an organization that rights wrongs." Leah shrugged. "I'm sure none of you are angels but I learned enough from my father to know that sometimes justice cannot be realized through the normal channels. I think Pytheon is an abnormal channel."

That was one way of describing what they did, who they were. It was simplistic but she'd nailed it. Leah bit the corner of her lip and Seth knew she wanted to say more. "I think your working life is full of puzzles, intrigue, hard decisions, and possible danger. In light of that, is it possible that you are reading too much into this situation with your father?"

Where was she going with this?

"Maybe there was a mix-up with his death, maybe you did get the wrong information. Maybe he's just finally found a way to contact you, through me, and is taking it. Maybe you're..."

Seth waited for her to finish her sentence, suspecting he knew what she was about to say.

"Overreacting?"

Yep, there it was. Seth forced himself not to look impatient, not to dismiss her concern with a scathing retort. He loved civilians and their rosy, let's look on the bright side of life, attitude. No, he was not overreacting, yes, this situation was weird. He had a pseudo-father who'd popped up out of nowhere and a missing teenager taken by The Recruiter and both incidents happened in Cape Town. Coincidence? He didn't think so, it was all too damned convenient.

Seth opened his mouth to explain, shut it again, and shook his head.

Leah sighed and pushed herself away from the kitchen counter. "It was just an idea, my two cents' worth. I can see you don't want to discuss this—"

Damn straight.

"And you must be longing for that shower. Let me show

you your room."

Seth followed Leah up the stairs onto the first floor and she opened the door to the first door on her right. "This is the guest room; my room is across the hall."

Seth entered the room, white and gray, dominated by a massive bed. God, it looked so damned comfortable. Then he imagined Leah in that bed with him and a little of his exhaustion disappeared. Yeah, if she offered, he could muster up the energy. Seth dropped his pack on the floor and removed the Glock from the hollow in his back and ignored Leah's gasp of surprise. He checked that the safety was on and placed it into the drawer of the nightstand. He removed the top of his beer bottle and took a long, long sip.

"God, that tastes like heaven," he murmured, resting the cool bottle against his throbbing forehead.

"I'll leave you to it. Dinner in thirty minutes?"

"Thanks."

As she walked away, Seth fought the urge to ask her about the kiss they shared in that cell, how she remembered it and whether she ever thought about it, whether she ever thought about him. Because the hell of it was that none of the women he'd ever had sex with managed to rock his boat like Leah did. And all they'd done was kiss…

Leah's kiss had been soft, exploratory, emotional. Oh, she'd been upset but when he kissed her she managed to temporarily forget she was in a cell, why she'd been arrested, and that she was married to a douchebag. And, conversely, that kiss had taken him away; it had been a temporary holiday from the stresses of his job and the busy but lonely life he'd chosen. He'd felt like he could kiss her all night, like she was the one woman he could consider kissing for the rest of...

Seth scrubbed his face with his hands. He was overtired if he was thinking about Leah in terms of the rest of his life. He reminded himself that close relationships made him feel overwhelmed because, thanks to living with an overprotective mother, he deeply feared feeling emotion, good and bad. His lack of stability and fear he experienced as a child had led to him learning to detach from his feelings. He was very self-sufficient and was a master at compartmentalizing his life. In his job, he had to be.

Leah was both work and temptation. She'd been pulled into this game for a reason he had yet to determine and he had to protect her and, at the same time, had to protect himself, his heart, and his steady, stable life.

And in between figuring out who this shadowy figure who called himself his father was, he also had a boy to find. He'd visited the Khans earlier that day and had touched base with the worried family. Cracker was currently analyzing all the computers in the house and tomorrow he was going to talk to Fayed's sister, his schoolmates, and other friends. Someone knew something...

But for now he was going to finish his beer, have a shower, and grab some food. He wouldn't say no to some great sex but that wasn't on the menu.

Sadly.

MUCH LATER IN her bedroom, Leah tossed the book she'd been trying to read onto the bed and yanked a pile of work folders towards her. Her thoughts, as they had all evening, wandered to Seth and she wondered what he was doing.

He was sleeping, idiot. He'd wolfed down dinner, told her he needed to work and, after helping her clean up the kitchen, headed upstairs, leaving her to fill a couple of hours before bedtime. Hours that had dragged without company...his company.

Leah shoved her hands into her hair and tugged, frustrated with herself. *You had your heart stomped on two and a bit weeks ago and you're thinking about another man?* It was replacement thinking, transference, a way for her not to think about Heath and the hurt he'd inflicted on her. And Seth was as perfect for that since he was absolutely nothing like her ex-fiancé, husband...she didn't know what to call him. Thinking about Seth was a way to avoid dealing with the breakup. Seth was Heath's complete opposite; tough and terse where Heath was gentler and more pliable. Seth was ultra-alpha, Heath was as beta as they came. Seth was passion, Heath was safety. They were, on every level, so very different and that had to be why she was thinking of Seth so much, even going as far as to consider him a perfect rebound guy, a wonderful way to get over her split from her husband who never was and her broken heart.

But...her heart wasn't really broken. She felt humiliated and blindsided, but was she as upset and devastated as she should be? Probably not.

If she was so in love with Heath as she'd always professed

to be, shouldn't she be crying more, ranting and raving? If she was so crazy in love with her husband, should she be feeling a little relieved, like she'd been given an emotional, as well as a literal, get out of jail free card?

Okay, she definitely needed to think about this a little more. And she needed to stop thinking about Mr. Rock-Hard-Abs-and-Sexy-Biceps a whole lot less.

"Leah?"

Leah jumped at Seth's voice and she spun around to look at her bedroom door. Leah eventually managed to croak out a sound that vaguely resembled a "yes?"

"I'm taking a walk around the house. I'll be back in five minutes." Seth told her through the closed door. Leah looked at her bedside clock; it was 11:05. Leah heard Seth's feet on the stairs and thought he was mad to go outside, hard rain pounded the roof and windows and a harsh wind caused the branches of the oak trees to scrape against the side of the house. Thunder rolled in after every lightning strike.

Leah looked down at a set of house plans and couldn't make sense of the floor plan. 11:10. *Get it together, Hamilton!* She pulled the hem of her t-shirt over her bended knees and stared at the clock, listening for Seth's footsteps on the stairs. Giving up her attempt at work, and irritated at her girlish bout of nerves, Leah walked over to her large window that looked over her pool.

Leah blinked, not sure whether her eyes were playing tricks on her. When she opened her eyes again, the body was still lying face down in her pool; dark head, broad shoulders, dark athletic shorts. Seth? Could it be?

Every atom in Leah's body froze as her mind started spinning. She banged her fist against the glass of the window so hard that the glass cracked. She screamed Seth's name and took off, yanking the bedroom door open and flying down the passage. She negotiated the stairs by the occasional burst of lightning. The fastest way to the pool was through the kitchen and she skidded across the tiles to the outside door. Her hands shaking, she attacked the handle of the kitchen door. After three attempts to open it, she finally registered that the door was locked and, after flipping the lock, she stumbled down the kitchen steps into the frigid rain.

"Please don't let him be dead, please don't let him be dead." She chanted as she hit the path that led around the house.

"Help!" she shouted but the wind carried her words away.

Running towards the pool, Leah shrieked when a warm arm wrapped around her waist and pulled her into a hard, hot, muscled body.

"What the hell are you doing?" Seth yelled in her ear, his words half swallowed by the wind.

Leah's legs collapsed as Seth spun her around and she snuggled into his chest, gripping him like a baby monkey. She considered yelling at him for scaring her half to death but she realized if she tried to talk, she might bite off her tongue because her teeth were chattering so much. It was safer to cling.

"And why are you half-naked?" Seth shouted as he scooped her up.

Skin to skin, she finally felt safe.

Safe and warm. Protected.

Leah hauled in some deep breaths as heat of Seth's body both warmed her up. She became aware of her bare inner thighs on Seth's skin, the ridges of his muscled body. He held her easily, his hand under her butt cheeks, his mouth bent to hers. Two minutes ago she'd been scared spitless, now she had wet panties and a racing heart and it was all because Seth was warm and strong and, God, so damn sexy.

The thought hit her with the power of a lightning bolt. If Seth was holding her then who was in the pool? Every muscle and tendon in her body stiffened. She pushed against Seth's chest and he looked at into her eyes, his expression puzzled.

"What now?"

"There's a body in the pool." Leah stated.

"I know. It's nothing to panic about."

There was a dead man in her pool. She thought she might be allowed to panic a little.

Seth dropped her to her feet but he held her elbows to make sure that she wouldn't fall over. He pushed his soaking hair off his forehead, looked towards the pool, and blew out a long breath. Seth held her hand as he led her to the edge of the pool. The pale, lifeless figure was still floating in the deep end of the pool but up close Leah noticed it looked too lifeless, too rigid.

She placed a hand on her heart and breathed again. "It's a mannequin."

Seth nodded and walked around to other side of the

pool. Going down on his haunches, he stretched out a hand and pulled the mannequin towards him, flipping it over when it reached the side of the pool. It was a male mannequin, dressed in plain, black swimming shorts. It had wide shoulders and a fake six pack and when Seth grabbed its head, a dark brown wig came away in his hand. Seth tossed the wig aside, hauled the dummy out and laid it on the tiles. He stood up, placed his hands on his hips, and looked down. After a few moments, his eyes locked on hers.

"So, is finding a life-size, life-like mannequin in pool something that happens often around here?"

Leah instantly recognized the sound of the front door to the guest house door opening but before she could turn or even think of calling out a greeting, Seth had her behind his back and his right hand whipped his pistol out of the back of his shorts and he pointed it at Milo.

Milo instantly turned pale and lifted up his hands. "Whoa! What the hell? Leah?"

"Leah, you know this guy?" Seth didn't drop the gun or turn to look at her as he asked the question.

Leah moved so she was standing next to Seth and she placed his hand on his forearm in an attempt to get him to lower his weapon. Neither Seth's arm nor eyes wavered.

"Yes, I know him. Please put the gun down."

"How do you know him?" Seth demanded, his voice harsh.

"He's an old friend, my best friend. He rents the guest house from me." Leah explained.

"He the type who would put a mannequin in the pool?"

"No!" Leah replied, now thoroughly wet and miserable.

She placed her hands on her hips and glared at Seth who, finally and far too slowly, lowered his weapon, holding it against his thigh.

"What the hell is going on, Leah? Who's the dickhead?" Milo demanded, trying to sound tough but failing.

"I'm the dickhead still holding the gun," Seth replied in a menacing voice.

Leah closed her eyes and shook her head. She'd had enough. She was wet and cold and scared and irritated and turned on. An altogether too uncomfortable state of affairs. "Milo, this is Seth, I'll explain who and what he is doing here in the morning."

Milo frowned. "Okay. And are you also going to explain why there's a dead guy next to the pool?"

Leah narrowed her eyes at him. Milo was prone to drama and, by tomorrow, he'd have a wonderful—and far from truthful—account of tonight to share with his friends.

"It's a mannequin, Mi, as you well know. I'm going to bed."

Ignoring Seth, who fell into step beside her, she walked back into the house and up the stairs to her bedroom. At the door to her room, Seth placed a hand on her shoulder and she slowly turned around. She lifted her eyes to meet his. His expression was part annoyance, part amusement, all frustration.

"Did you want to say something, Halcott?" she asked when he just looked at her, his eyes starting at her feet and leisurely making her way upwards.

Seth placed his hand on the doorframe above her head and the muscles in his chest and abdomen rippled with movement. God, the man was beautifully ripped.

"A couple of things…" His eyes hardened and darkened as he turned into Officer Commanding on her. "You should have stayed in the house, where you were relatively safe. And dry."

"I thought the mannequin was you." Leah protested.

"Still, you should've stayed inside." Seth lifted her chin with his finger and his fantastic eyes drilled into her again. "And if you ever touch my arm again when I am pointing a gun at someone I'll lose my shit, which is not something you want to see."

It took all her willpower to keep her eyes steady on his.

"Are we clear?" Seth asked, his voice soft but steady, determined.

Leah tipped her head and nodded. "Yeah. Forgive me for being worried that you were face down in my pool," she muttered.

"I'm pretty hard to kill, Leah. And I suggest you get out of that wet t-shirt before you catch a cold…"

Leah looked down and saw the white shirt was plastered against her chest, showing off her boobs and her cold and puckered nipples. Shit, she thought, blushing. She steeled herself to meet Seth's eyes but when she finally did the door to his room was closing. Thank God.

Chapter Three

"PRETTIEST RUN I think I've ever done."

Leah turned her head to look at Seth and smiled. They were on the promenade, heading back to her house via the village of St. James and he was looking at the iconic and brightly colored bathing boxes on the mostly empty beach. Waves broke over the wall of the tidal pool and a fishing boat was heading out to sea.

They'd both needed this. Despite a night short on sleep—the little she'd managed curled up in the chair in the corner of her room—she'd invited Seth to run with her and he'd quickly agreed. Like her, he seemed to need to stretch his muscles, to distance himself from the craziness of the night before.

Someone had tossed a mannequin in her swimming pool. Why? It was a sick joke, a malicious prank. Oh Lord, she hoped that was all it was.

They slowed down and Seth hit a button on his watch as he stopped. He placed two fingers on the pulse point on his neck and looked out to sea. "There's a whale at twoo'clock," he said, his eyes flicking between his watch and the horizon. "Quite far out. I saw a splash."

Hauling in air, Leah placed her hands on her hips and

stared out to sea and within twenty seconds she saw the whale's plume and a flash of the tail thumping the surface of the ocean. God, she loved Cape Town, loved the weather, and her scenic surroundings. The sea and the sun, the wonderful combination of Africa and Europe, of new world and old.

"It's a long way from New York." Seth quietly stated, dropping his hand.

"I love New York but here, at the end of the day, I can take a glass of wine onto the veranda and watch the sea. This is, well, home. It has been since the first day I arrived here, fifteen years ago." Now that was too much information, chatty-Cathy. She wondered why she had little control over her mouth around him. He had a way of pulling her words to the surface, of looking at her, his amazing eyes encouraging her to talk.

Dammit. She would be far happier if she could just dismiss him as being another good-looking guy who'd dropped into her life and who would disappear again in a week or so. She didn't want to be intrigued by him, turned on by him.

But she was.

He was a temporary Band-Aid for her heart, a distraction, someone and something thing else to focus on besides Heath and her non-marriage. He, it, Seth, didn't mean anything.

"Did you run with Heath?" Seth demanded, grabbing the railing with his hands and stretching his calf muscles.

And really, in that position, how was she not supposed to look at his butt?

Seth turned his head and looked her, his expression expectant. What had he asked? Oh, right…Heath.

"Heath, run?" She scoffed. "Heath didn't exercise much. Or at all."

Seth pulled his left arm across his chest to hold it with his right arm. The movement caused his shirt to pull tight across his stomach and she could see the ridges of that impressive abdominal pack. Leah felt the moisture disappear from her mouth and sighed. Seth had the ability to rocket her from nun to give-me-some in ten seconds flat.

Leah held her right ankle against her butt cheek, stretching out her quadriceps. Seth swallowed and looked out to sea. Mm, so maybe she wasn't the only one who liked what they saw. It was just lust, a normal run of the mill attraction.

He was rebound guy.

"Jed said that he wanted a hefty chunk of change from you."

Leah wrinkled her nose, annoyance replacing lust. "We had a pre-nup and since our marriage only lasted a few hours, my lawyer walked the floor with his lawyer. He received nothing, will receive nothing…in fact, I don't want a divorce, I want an annulment."

"Good for you." Seth looked down at his hand. "Damn, it should've been his face."

Say what? Leah narrowed her eyes. "Explain that cryptic statement, Halcott."

Seth's innocent expression needed a great deal of work.

"What did you do to Heath? You did something, didn't you?" Leah persisted.

Seth took another long moment before answering her. "Your brother and I made it clear to Green how unamusing we found his behavior."

Leah lifted her fist to her lips and looked at him with horrified eyes. "You beat him up?"

"We made it clear that we didn't appreciate his behavior."

Leah groaned. "Oh, God, you did! You worked him over."

Seth didn't confirm or deny. Or apologize. Not that she expected him to do either.

"He could've laid assault charges against you!"

"He's not that brave," Seth said, his words confirming that he, and her brother, had done something to Heath.

And with their special ops training and skills, "something" could range from a punch to water-torture. She wanted to feel bad for Heath but she just couldn't get there. She wasn't a saint, for goodness sake.

"We made our point." Seth raised his hand and waved the subject away.

Leah rested her forearms on the railing. "That explains so much. I did some damage to the room and when my lawyer approached the hotel so I could pay for the damages; he was told that Heath settled the bill."

Seth smiled. "Mmm, you did a damn good job destroying that room. The bill maxed out both his savings and credit cards."

"You made him settle the bill?"

She saw the amusement in his eyes. "We didn't make

him do anything. We just made a strong suggestion."

Leah snorted. "Strong suggestion my ass."

"It's a very pretty ass," Seth agreed, his gazemoving from her eyes, to her butt and back up again. "You're pretty, all over."

Seth's hand lifted and his fingers encircled her throat, his thumb tracing the tight cords in her neck. "When I kissed you two weeks ago I wanted to distract you, to take your mind off the situation."

"It worked," Leah admitted, her eyes locked on his, fascinated by the way his eyes moved from moss to hunter green and back again.

"This time it has nothing to do with distraction, with making you feel better. This is about what I want," Seth murmured, moving to close the gap between them.

He stopped a fraction from her and she couldn't help stepping into his space, pushing her breasts into his hard chest, sliding her smooth calf against his bigger, rougher leg. Leah's breath hitched. His fingers moved up and down her neck and created a path of white light straight to her groin. She was shocked at how much she wanted him to move his hand up to her breast, to find her sensitive nipples through the thin layers of cotton. She should step away, but she was so enjoying the heat of his body, his hardness of his broad chest, the power in the arms that held her.

She should ease herself back into dating and sex. Going from Heath and his betrayal to Seth, in the space of two and a half weeks with no one in between, was like skipping basic parachute training to throwing herself from short buildings with a tiny 'chute.

Leah found herself staring into a hard shoulder as his hands gripped her hips. At his silent command, she lifted her face and stared into his amazing eyes. Heat and desire churned within them and his fingers pressed into the flesh on her hips. He wanted her…and for a brief instant she felt powerful and invincible.

She wasn't sad or humiliated or feeling less than…Seth wanted her and it felt good.

Seth's mouth settled on hers, as powerful as a tsunami and as gentle as a butterfly's kiss. His lips were cool but insistent, his tongue flickering between hers, persistent but undemanding. *Here I am, taste me, know me.* It was primal, instinctive, searching.

She lost time in his arms. She could have been there for hours or seconds. Time and its silly rules held no meaning. There was just this man and his clever lips and his hard, strong, safe haven of a body.

When Seth finally pulled away from her mouth, she rested the side of her face on his shoulder and listened to his heartbeat. There was something curiously intimate listening to someone's life force pump in their chest.

It was even more intimate than the rigidity of his erection pressing into her stomach.

"I want you," he said.

He wanted her. It was a simple, powerful statement. Leah pulled back and forced herself to look up at him, trying to think. They had crackling chemistry and she wanted, desperately, to get naked with him but she was a little scared, a lot hesitant. Sleeping with Seth wasn't a good idea and not only because, up until a few weeks ago, she'd been in a committed, long-term relationship that had ended in dreadful circumstances. Apart from those very good reasons not to do this, Seth wasn't just another arbitrary man, he wasn't someone she could have some fun with and forget about. He was her brother's best friend. They would be in each other's lives for a long time to come. Sleeping together now would cause some awkwardness in the future; she wasn't sure if she could attend future family gatherings—Seth was Jed's family as much as she was—and know that she'd had hot, fantastic sex with the man across the table.

Because it would be hot and it would be frickin' fantastic and she couldn't imagine *not* wanting a repeat performance.

His future wife/girlfriend/partner might object.

Leah opened her mouth to speak, having no idea what she intended to say, when Seth dropped his hands from her body and moved back, creating some distance between them. Distance they needed but she didn't want. Judging by the impressive erection tenting his athletic shorts, neither did he.

"I shouldn't say that, neither should I be kissing you. There are reasons why that isn't a good idea."

"Such as?"

"You are recovering from a crappy couple of weeks and that's reason enough for us not to be doing this. But, apart from that, I've got a lot to deal with...I have a Pytheon case to solve and that's hard enough without some imposter taking you to lunch and someone tossing mannequins in your pool." Seth pushed his fingers through his hair and released a long stream of air.

"Someone is using you to get to me and I need to stay sharp. I need to focus on that and finding..." He hesitated, pulled a face, and looked towards the bright bathing boxes. "I just need to concentrate and you are a distraction."

Leah sighed. Like Jed and her dad, who was a retired general in the US Army, Seth had too many secrets and was far too proficient at keeping them. All three were non-communicative and emotionally unavailable, at least Jed had been until he'd met McKenna. Leah was used to secrets. She'd lived with them all her life.

Besides, she and Seth were just strangers experiencing a chemical reaction and she had no right to explanations.

He was right, they shouldn't do this, *should not do this.* That chemical reaction could, very easily, blow up in their faces. Frankly, she'd had enough emotional explosions lately to last a lifetime.

Besides, in a normal world—and her world right now was anything but normal—a man like Seth, someone who fascinated her as much as he did had the power to hurt her, the ability to turn her well-ordered, stable life upside down. When she was fully over her breakup, she'd be glad she didn't complicate matters with Seth. She knew this.

After all, the best cheese was always found in mousetraps.

Leah gave herself a mental slap and pulled a bright, fake smile onto her face. "Let's head for home. I'm starving. Are you starving?" She started to walk towards home, her heart heavy and her mouth dry with disappointment.

She turned her head to look back at him and he took a

while to move his eyes from her butt to herface.

"You have no damned idea how much," he muttered as he started to follow her home.

Dammit. Instinctively, she knew that he wasn't thinking of food.

★ ★ ★

SETH WAS EXCEPTIONALLY good at compartmentalizing his life, his work, his thoughts and emotions but as they walked back to the house, those carefully constructed boxes he'd created were falling apart. He needed to think of Leah as work, a part of a puzzle he had to solve but she was also need, and heat, and want. She was Jed's sister and therefore someone he felt the need to protect yet she also heated his blood and fried his common sense.

He wanted her but he didn't want to want her…honestly, he was deeply uncomfortable with how she made him feel. He liked women, he did. He liked the way they moved, laughed, thought. They were sensitive and tangled, sweet smelling and softer but he liked them in small doses.

He was, essentially, a loner and too much personal time spent with one person made him scratchy. Dinner and sex was normally as much "together" time as he could handle yet he found Leah easy to be around and ridiculously difficult to resist.

She was a unique combination of brains and heart and sexiness. And it was her sexy that was killing him—but she was vulnerable and sad and looking for an escape. God knew he wasn't an angel but he did try to not be a complete bastard either.

He needed to get his head back in the game. Across town there was a family whose world had been flipped upside down and he had to try and trace who was playing this cat-and-mouse-and-mannequin game with him and why.

The why was the question that buzzed around his head. Could it be his father? Not likely but, if it was, why had he faked his death? What was his aim, his payoff, his motive?

When he'd heard about Ben's death, he'd easily accepted the news. There had been no reason to doubt the Spring PD. The burnt body in the car was the same age, build, and ethnicity as his father and the car was registered to him. Personal effects had been found next to his body. Seth stopped, stared at the road, and rubbed the back of his neck. Death was easy to fake. He'd done it once or ten times himself. Yeah, he was a professional but anyone with a modicum of intelligence could, especially in an area with an underfunded, under resourced, and inexperienced police department, like Spring, get away with it.

"What's wrong?"

Seth shook his head, his brain spinning.

Was his father out there? The law of probability told him there was a chance that he was. So that begged the question…if so, why? What the hell did he want?

Me. He wanted what he always wanted, the one thing he never had. He wanted me. His son, his heir, the fruit of his loins.

Screw that. Not going to happen.

Leah looked at him, her blue eyes troubled. "Want to tell me what conclusion you came to?"

"What makes you think—"

"Seth, I'm not a ditsy girl without a brain in her head." Leah interrupted him. "You came to a conclusion back there and I want to know what it is. I have a right to know what you're thinking, especially since I'm neck-deep in whatever craziness I've been dropped into."

Leah stopped, turned to face him, and drilled a sharp tipped finger into his chest. Seth covered her small hand with his and sighed when heat radiated into his hands and up his arm. Shit. This was so damned inconvenient.

Leah just lifted both her eyebrows and waited, her eyes demanding a truthful answer.

Seth sighed and capitulated. "I think that there is a possibility, a very small possibility, that your lunch companion might, actually, be my father. And he's playing games with us."

Leah tipped her head to one side. "You said that he died in a car crash."

"Maybe." Seth took her hand and felt the hair on the back of his neck rise.

He looked down and goose bumps peppered his skin and he knew, he simply knew, someone was watching him. He tugged Leah to his chest, banded his arm around her and turned slowly, his eyes scanning the quiet road, the houses around them. The road was empty of parked cars and while there were people around, no one looked suspicious.

Was he overreacting? Was he seeing shadows when there were none? Was it because this was about his father and anything to do with that waste of DNA human being colored his thoughts? He didn't know but he needed to find out, soon.

Seth felt his phone vibrate within its cover attached to his left bicep and he pulled the device out, swiping his thumb across the screen. He greeted Stone and he grabbed Leah's hand and started to walk. The sooner they got home, the happier he'd be.

"How's it going, Seth?" Stone's deep voice reverberated in his ear.

"It's going. I'm meeting with the Khans again later this morning," Seth answered him.

"The Khans?" Leah asked.

Seth ignored her.

"I'm concerned that your focus is fractured and you can't do justice to either investigation," Stone said, worry in his voice.

"Stone, I routinely juggle more than a couple balls in the air, I can handle this," Seth replied, his tone terse.

Leah tugged his hand to get him to look at her. When he did, she frowned. "What's going on? Who are you talking to?"

"Sounds like you have your hands full." Stone drawled. "It that Leah?"

He wished his hands were full of her. *Focus, Halcott.* "Yeah," Seth sourly replied.

"Interesting." Stone drawled. "Oh, before I forget, I'm

sending someone to help you. He's a new hire. An ex-Marine with some serious sniping and hacking skills."

"I don't need help." Seth growled.

Stone ignored his statement. "He'll be with you in a couple of days."

There was no point in arguing, Stone had made up his mind. And it was his prerogative to send his employees wherever the hell he wanted to. Dammit.

"Name?" Seth demanded.

"Jett Smith-Jones."

Well, that was interesting. He instantly recognized the name. After a series of particularly audacious rescues of hostages from extremist camps in south Yemen and Syria, JSJ and his team were well respected in the spec ops community. Seth wondered why he'd left the military. It could be as simple as wanting to extend his life expectancy or as complex as PSTD. His brow furrowed. Yes, Stone had the right to hire whom he wanted but the agents took their orders from Seth and he liked having a say in the process. Not knowing who was on his team made him feel antsy and out of control.

"Trust me, Seth," Stone said, reading his mind.

Seth sighed. He did. He just trusted himself and his instincts more. "We said we needed more people and you found one. I can live with that." He told Stone.

"Liar," Stone cheerfully replied. "You hate the idea of someone being on the books, under your control, who you haven't met and vetted."

"Yeah, well...Look, I don't need him here," Seth said as he and Leah approached the gate to her house.

"You might in the future," Stone replied as Leah pulled out the remote that opened the wrought iron gate "I've got another call coming in. I'll let you know Jett's ETA."

The electric gate to Leah's property opened and they walked up the driveway. Leah pulled her hand out of his and his instantly felt empty. What the hell was wrong with him?

Apart from being horny, tired, stressed, and frustrated?

He didn't have a clue.

Chapter Four

"YO, LEE!"

Leah was about to run up the stairs to shower and change when she heard a familiar voice shouting a greeting from the kitchen. Hell, Milo. She needed to explain about last night, explain why he had the bad end of a gun pointed at his head. Leah's shoulders slumped. Milo would be shocked and then he would go into protective mode and dealing with Seth, who took protectiveness to art form, was hard enough.

Milo was her business partner and best friend and he knew her inside out. He would instantly pick up on the tension between her and Seth and would quickly realize their attraction was off the charts. Then Milo would get in her face, demanding answers to questions she didn't want him to ask, telling her to man up and girl up and do something to, with, the hot man who'd landed in her metaphorical lap.

Milo had no understanding of the word "discreet" or the phrase "minding his own business."

Leah stepped through the door into the kitchen and walked up to Milo and placed her arms around his waist, lifting her lips to kiss his cheek.

Milo placed his big hand against her face and pushed her

away. "Ugh, stop with the affection."

"Are you okay?"

Milo squinted down at her. "Well, on the plus side, I don't have any bullet holes in me but I'm still a bit freaked out." Milo stepped back to look down into her face. "Okay, what's going on? And why is sexy Seth here?"

Leah darted a look behind her and sighed. Seth was still in the hallway on his phone and looking tough and hot—dear Lord, so hot!—and perfectly pissed.

"Long story," Leah said, keeping her voice low.

"You sleeping with him?"

Leah, her hand still on his waist, grabbed some skin and twisted. Milo yelped like a girl.

"No."

Milo rubbed his side. "But you want to. Since that night in jail you've wanted to get jiggy with him."

Leah wrinkled her nose. "Gross."

Milo grinned. "It shouldn't be, not if you do it properly and he looks like a dude who knows his way around a woman's—"

Leah slammed a fist into his arm. "Shut up!"

"Are you really telling me that the dildo I bought you as a sorry-your-wedding-night-sucked present is preferable to *him*?"

Well, no. Leah blushed as Milo cocked an eyebrow at her and waited for her response. Leah wanted to lie, wanted to act casual, wanted to dig a hole in the sand and bury her head in it but she couldn't. Milo wouldn't let her.

"It's not like that," she muttered.

"Oh, it's so like that and you so want to. Good. Discounting the fact that he pointed a loaded weapon at me, he looks like he could be a perfect rebound guy. Someone to get you back into the saddle."

And, as she'd expected, there it was.

"I'm not sure I want to get back in the saddle!" Leah hissed.

"Sure you do."

Milo put his arm around her shoulders as Seth walked into the kitchen. Seth lifted his eyebrows at the intimate gesture and within seconds Milo dropped his arm and, to his credit, thrust his hand in Seth's direction and introduced himself. They were so different. Both were tall but Milo had the long, wiry body of the rock climber and distance runner he was while Seth was just big, everywhere.

Leah remembered the feel of his big "everywhere" plastered against her stomach and swallowed, trying to get some moisture back into her mouth.

"Sorry about last night," Seth said to Milo before frowning at Leah. "Leah forgot to mention that she rented the guest house."

"Yeah, we just sold my flat so I'm staying here while I look for a new place. Leah and I partner on certain projects and I run the accounting side of her business." Milo, being Milo, headed directly for her fridge. He opened the door and sent Leah a baleful look. "Leah, there's food but none of it is organic. Can you please buy decent food?"

Milo nagged her continuously about her eating habits and Leah silently thanked him for this little piece of normality. She needed normal.

Leah pointed a finger at Milo. "If you're making breakfast do not make me drink one of your super healthy, super yuck smoothies. They are disgusting."

"Yeah, but good for you." Milo retorted and snapped his head around to narrow his eyes at Seth. "Do you believe in eating healthily?"

"I believe in eating," Seth said, the twitch at the corner of his mouth indicating that he was amused.

"Heathens," Milo muttered, pulling a pack of bacon out of the fridge. After looking at Seth, he pulled out another. Eggs and mushrooms followed the bacon onto the counter.

"So, do you often come over and cook Leah breakfast?" Seth asked, his tone casual but Leah could feel the tension radiating off him.

Why? What was his problem?

Milo smiled as he grabbed a pan from the cupboard beneath the expensive gas stove. "Sure. Sometimes I just stumble down the stairs and cook breakfast."

Seth stiffened and Leah sighed, finally catching on. "Stop making trouble, Milo." She turned to Seth. "Milo and I have been friends since school."

Seth relaxed a fraction and Leah couldn't tell if he'd asked the question because he was jealous or because he was trying to make sense of their relationship. Probably, the latter. Seth, with his shuttered eyes and implacable expression, didn't seem the type to get jealous. Annoyed that she was allowing him to get to her, she walked around the island counter and headed for the coffee machine.

She pulled cups down and lifted one in the air. "Who would like a cup?" she asked.

Seth and Milo nodded. Leah busied herself at the coffee machine, wishing she could forget about the kiss she and Seth shared. It had been, unfortunately, equally amazing, perhaps even more panty-melting than the jail kiss. She really wanted to explore his amazing body. He'd taken his shirt off on their run and she nearly ran into a light post because she'd been so busy gawking. He had the most perfect build, not overly muscled but immensely fit and powerful. Fast.

Leah was familiar with the aboriginal tattoo around his bicep but she'd caught another glimpse of the top of a tattoo on his hip and wished she could lower his pants to discover what it was.

Oh, who was she kidding? She was curious about his tattoo but it wasn't why she really wanted to drop his pants. He didn't… no, that wasn't right; he *wouldn't* take her to bed and fulfill about a hundred fantasies. Because he thought she was too vulnerable, heartbroken, damaged.

How could she tell him, without actually telling him, that all she could think about was how loudly he could make her scream?

"Lee?"

Milo's fingers snapping an inch from her nose made her jerk back.

She slapped his hand away. "What?"

Milo held her bright blue phone out to her. "Philippe sent you a text message confirming your date at Minx tonight."

"It's not a date-date." Leah snatched her phone from his hand. "And will you please stop reading my text messages?"

"I'm nosy, you know that." Milo shrugged, not in the least apologetic. "You might not think it's a date but he's hoping he can get lucky."

Leah glared at her friend. "What are you talking about?"

"He's hoping to comfort you, to help you move on. And by moving on, I mean that he wants to take you to bed." Milo's lips twitched as he sent Seth a side look. "I'm not morally opposed to you having a rebound fling but not with him."

"Shut up, Milo," Leah said, blushing furiously.

"I'd like you to cancel your dinner arrangement." Seth's words were low and while his words suggested he was making a request, she heard the command in his voice. She looked at him and saw his eyes on hers. He lifted a hand. "I can see that you want to argue but let's not, okay? Will you postpone this arrangement? Just until we have a better handle on the situation?"

Dammit, why did he have to sound so damn reasonable?

"What is the situation?" Milo asked. "What's going on?"

"Leah? You willing to postpone?" Seth asked her, folding his big arms against his chest.

"I'm not trying to be difficult but what you"—she pointed at Milo—"are forgetting and what Seth doesn't know is that Philippe is a client, an influential client. My refusing to have dinner would be a slap in his face. I can't afford to do that." She looked at Seth. "I'll ask him to collect me and I'll take a taxi home. I promise I'll be fine."

Seth shook his head. "You are a part of whatever is going on here and I can't be sure if you have a target on your pretty ass or not." Seth drawled, his eyes not leaving her face. He nodded to the phone still in her hand. "Please call him and cancel."

Cancel not postpone. She was so damn tempted. "Seth, I really can't. I need to do this."

Seth pinched the bridge of his nose. "I get that this is frustrating for you…"

"You have no freakin' idea," Leah muttered and their eyes clashed and his heated. Did he know she wasn't only referring to his fake father and the mannequin in the pool?

"Will someone tell me what's going on?"

Leah drilled Milo with a "not now" look. "Seth, I genuinely believe that I will be okay." Leah insisted. "I'll be in a public place. I'll find an excuse to leave early—"

Seth shook his head and looked resigned. "You go, I go. You'll have to meet him there and you'll leave with me. Are we clear on that?"

Leah thought about challenging his terse statements, considered arguing but she quickly realized she'd won a major argument. She thought she should quit while she was ahead.

"Deal," she quickly agreed before Seth could change his mind.

"Will someone tell me what is going on?" Milo demanded.

Seth sent Leah another hot look before picking up his coffee cup and heading for the hall. "Leah can fill you in. I'm going to shower and dress. Yell when breakfast is ready."

★ ★ ★

SETH LOOKED ACROSS the expensively decorated room to where Leah was sitting between Fayed's mother and sister, looking down at the photo album on her lap. Fatima Khan had a tissue in her hand and frequently wiped the tears from her eyes and Fayed's sister stared at the Persian carpet with a blank-eyed stare. Leah was rubbing big circles on her back.

After breakfast, Seth explained where they were going and why and Leah was, initially, shocked. After she'd asked a couple of intelligent, salient questions about Fayed's disappearance, she'd asked him how she could help.

He'd asked her to engage with the mother and sister and she'd done that with warmth and unforced empathy. She'd pulled them over to the couch and asked to see pictures of Fayed, which Fatima had been happy to show her. Leah's presence had allowed him to pull Ismail Khan into the study for another question and answer session. Unfortunately he didn't have any new information to add to the little he had.

Fayed was obsessed with computers. Then why didn't he take his laptop with him? Fayed was a loner with no friends. He had friends; his family just didn't know them. He loved his family; he would never hurt his mother like this. Except he was doing exactly that.

Seth took a cup of coffee from Ismail and nodded when the still dignified gentleman asked to be excused to take a call. He'd done all he could here; Seth decided, he had tracers on the phones, a couple of illegal listening devices placed in high traffic areas in case there was something the family wasn't telling him and Cracker was monitoring all the computers and tablets in the house. If something happened in the house, the alert would go to Seth's phone.

He'd made contact with a local operative, the same man who'd supplied him with his weapons and his bag of tricks, and he was using his contacts to source intel. On both Fayed and Seth's fake father.

After this meeting, he would leave Leah at her office, with strict instructions not to leave, and visit the local mosque and meet the Imam. After that he'd canvas hotels and B&Bs, looking for where fake-Ben had stayed while he was in Cape Town. In a tourist town, that was going to be a long and tedious process.

Maybe he'd get lucky but he wasn't holding his breath. Wearisome but it had to be done.

Leah was handling all of this well, he realized as he walked back into the formal lounge. Then again, she was the daughter of one of the highest ranking officers in the US military and her brother was a kick-ass operative. It was in her genes; he'd dropped into her life, flipped it upside down, yet she was rolling with the punches.

Oh, she wasn't wholly convinced she was in danger but she was smart enough to respect his training and his experience. Because she was a civilian, she kept forgetting that someone had gone to a lot of effort to snag his attention, had risked their life—or at least the limb Seth would've ripped off had he caught them—to play a nasty trick by dropping a mannequin in her pool. The UNSUB's actions should tell her, warn her to be cautious but the sexy woman preferred to look on the bright side of life.

He wished he could get a handle on her, put her into a box, work out what made her tick. He thought he'd figured out a little—losing her mother at such a young age would have had a massive impact on her and that being left with an austere father and a strong-willed brother, both determined to look after her, would be smothering. No wonder she'd run straight into the arms of the one person who was, in a million ways, different from her arrogant, strong, and conservative male relatives. She'd subconsciously chosen someone completely opposite to the men in her life… and a fat lot of good that had done her.

Subconscious choice or not, what had she seen in Heath with his preppy suits and soft mouth and hands? His pretentious accent and manicured fingernails? Yet what was Seth? An embittered ex-soldier with blood on his hands, a questionable bloodline, and a cynical outlook on life? Someone destined to be alone and to stay alone, someone obsessed with using his wits and brains, and sometimes his brawn, to extract people and stuff from sticky situations? Someone who knew that not all wrongs could be righted and not all justice could be found and that life frequently didn't make sense.

It wasn't like he was the catch of the century.

Even if could imagine a relationship with anyone—which he couldn't—Leah was way out of his league. Ignoring the fact that she was sliding out of a relationship, that she was hurt and confused and trying to find her feet…Ignoring all that as well as the fact he wasn't relationship material, would he be any better for her than asshat Heath? Oh, he wouldn't lie to Leah, or cheat on her, but he believed he wasn't a prize. He didn't communicate well, preferring to keep all his emotions bottled up inside. Work wise, he carried an enormous amount of responsibility and he often made decisions that changed lives. Those decisions could affect the lives of his agents, a community, a village, a city. A country. His work was important and he mostly enjoyed it. But parts of it stained his soul.

Annoyed by his introspection Seth placed his coffee cup on the table and willed Leah to look at him. Within ten seconds, she lifted her eyes and met his and something—a mixture of heat and desire and understanding—flashed between them. Sensing he wanted to leave, Leah nodded quickly and flipped the album closed and placed it on the table in front of her. She stood up and bent over Fatima Khan, giving her a quick hug and whispering something encouraging in her ear. Leah repeated the action with Fayed's sister.

She was warm and empathetic and kind. Those were traits he didn't come across often in his line of work. And damn, they were almost as sexy as her tiny waist, long legs, and perfect breasts.

She's trouble. Big, fat, messy trouble. Squared.

LEAH IMAGINED SINKING her head into her crème brûlée.

On the boredom scale of one to ten, Philippe rated a hundred and twenty seven. Leah sighed as she lifted her cup of espresso to her lips. She now had a precise breakdown of all the properties he owned throughout the world, a detailed description of every piece of art he'd ever bought, sold, and bartered, and was even told the pedigrees of the Borzoi champions he'd bred and raised.

Since there was, simply, something so sexy about conversing in French across a dinner table, Leah was still disappointed that, despite the Gallic pronunciation of his name, he didn't speak French. That was just, well, wrong. As was this date. All their previous conversations had been business-like and she'd never thought Philippe could be so damn dull.

Shoot me now. She sighed as Philippe launched into a monologue detailing his extensive wine cellar.

"So, how often do you sneak into your cellar and enjoy a bottle?' she asked during a brief pause.

Philippe looked at her as if she'd suggested he stand on the table and strip. "The wines are for collecting, not drinking!"

Leah shrugged at his scandalous expression and wished she was anywhere but here. But preferably with Seth.

Philippe reached across the table to take her hand and Leah sighed. It was past time to bring this evening to an end.

She wished she could tell him she'd rather stick fire ants in her eyes than go on another date with him but she suspected he would take that badly. He might be an arrogant bore but they did business together and she didn't want to antagonize him. She'd need to let him down gently and in a way that was no threat to his ego…

Her mobile rang in her evening bag and Leah sent Philippe an apologetic smile.

She yanked her phoneout and frowned at the display. Seth.

"You done?" he demanded, his voice rough and sexy in her ear.

Leah flashed Philippe a small smile and shrugged her shoulders apologetically and launched into a gabble of French. Neither Seth nor Philippe would understand but she could, at least, vent her frustration at him and the situation. "Yeah, this was a really bad idea. He's boring and annoying and he definitely wants to take me to bed to comfort me. That's a bit problematic since all I want to do is to go home and strip you naked and find out if sex can be as good as they say it can be."

There was a long silence on the other side of the phone before Seth replied in English. "Time to go, princess. My butt is numb and I'm tired of watching his ham-handed attempts at seducing you."

Leah quite liked the idea of emotionally erupting so she let loose with another gabble of fast French. "You just need to walk into a room and I want to climb you like a vine. How can I feel like this about you so soon after Heath? It makes no sense, I should be wailing and weeping. Yet, all I can think about is that you are so damn sexy and what you would feel like, in me"

"Je ressens la même chose."

He felt the same way. Leah pushed the tips of her fingers into her forehead. And…oh, *crapdammithell,* he spoke French! Oh…*shitohshitohshit.*

Leah placed her hand over her eye. "I think I want to die I'm so embarrassed." She whimpered. "How come you speak French? Why do you speak French?"

"If it helps, I also speak fluent Spanish, Farsi, Arabic and a smattering of Mandarin."

"Are you human?" Leah muttered.

Seth laughed. "I just have an ear for languages."

"Can we ignore what I just said?" Leah asked. Seth didn't reply so she assumed that was a solid "no."

"Where are you?" she eventually demanded, resting the backs of her bent fingers against her flushed cheeks. She'd blushed more around Seth that she had her entire life.

"I am watching your ass from these deeply uncomfortable bar stools while you eat lobster and flirt with that moron," Seth muttered. "Wrap it up…and why are we still speaking French?"

"Look, I know I've just made a huge fool of myself but can you extricate me from this situation?"

"Explain?"

"Hot hands, bad innuendos, wants to take me home."

"Just tell him you're not interested."

Leah sneaked a look at Philippe, who was stroking the inside of her wrist and looking impatient. "I don't want to offend him."

Seth sighed. "Sure. I'm coming in, act surprised to see me. I'm an old friend. We haven't seen each other in ages."

"Merci."

"You owe me."

Leah disconnected and sent Philippe one of her mega-watt smiles. "Sorry, about that."

Philippe waved her apology away and immediately launched into a long and boring story about shares he'd just purchased in new cell phone technology. Leah swiftly ate the rest of her crème Brûlée and she'd just finished her last spoonful when Seth entered the dining room and held a brief conversation with the maître d.

She faked her surprise and thought she was a damn good actress. "Why, that's Seth. Good grief!"

Philippe turned, looked at Seth and his back went steel straight. "Seth? Who is he to you?"

"An old family friend. I haven't seen him for years!" Leah laid her hand on her chest and fluttered her fingers. She didn't have to fake the appreciative look on her face as she took in his open neck black dress shirt, untucked and sleeves rolled up, the faded jeans and the scarred boots. Letting out an excited, feminine squeal, she bounded to her feet and, when he reached her, she wound her arms around his neck and lifted up on her scalpel-sharp heels to reach his mouth. She felt his hesitation, his jolt of surprise, and then his hands grasped hips and yanked her closer. His mouth took control of hers and the brief smooch she planned on giving him flipped over. Philippe and the restaurant faded away, and she and Seth…Seth's body, mouth, hands…were all that were important.

She'd never really been kissed before until Seth laid his

mouth on hers, Leah decided. He kissed with confidence, with...abundance. In addition to his strong hands, his firm lips, quick tongue, and hard body she felt like she'd landed in a place of utter safety, complete contentment. Nothing else mattered but living, owning, claiming this moment, this spot of time.

Nothing else could.

Seth broke the kiss and Leah teetered on her ridiculously high heels. *Note to self, do not kiss Seth when wearing heels.* The possibility of falling off the damn things was stratospheric. She dimly heard Seth introducing himself to Philippe, vaguely took in that Philippe was calling for the check, his face sullen and set.

Leah clutched Seth's arm and sent him a rueful look. Her smile faded as she picked up the heat in his eyes. Yeah, her earlier comments in French had ignited a firestorm within him and he was trying to talk himself out of walking her out of the restaurant and straight into his bed.

She wished he wouldn't; talk himself out of it that was. She wanted his heat, his fire. And not because she wanted to forget about Heath—God, since Seth's arrival she'd barely thought about him at all—her need for Seth was all about him and the craziness he ignited inside her.

Leah bit the inside of her lip. It didn't matter he wasn't long-term material, that he probably wasn't what she needed in a life partner—or what she thought she needed—that she couldn't visualize him in her life in even a casual way, but she felt like she needed to take this chemical connection to the wall, to roll with him, rage with him, shudder as she tipped into orgasm.

He was bad and bad for her. But, why was she so convinced she needed a little bad again?

Chapter Five

LEAH STEPPED ONTO the uneven pavement outside the restaurant and, annoyingly and again, felt unsteady on her scalpel-sharp heels. Grabbing Seth's sleeve for support, she found her footing and ambled towards her car, inhaling the clean scent of the summer squall that had blown through earlier. She ignored the exhaust fumes and food smells from the restaurants and concentrated on the combination of brine and rain and Seth's masculine cologne. She'd picked up vanilla and sandalwood, maybe a hint of citrus? Grapefruit? Lemon...

Jerked from her musings by a car passing through the puddle below the pavement, she grimaced as water soaked her heels and splashed her bare calves. Looking down, she cursed. Her suede, nude babies would now be permanently stained with mucky puddle water.

"Problem?"

Leah didn't bother to explain. Seth was so damn masculine; she didn't think he'd understand a woman's deep and abiding relationship with a special pair of designer shoes.

Leah tossed a glance up and sighed at his inscrutable expression. His hands were loose at his sides and his eyes were watching the street, the people, flicking over buildings and cars. He was prepared for anything but Leah knew, with one swipe of her mouth across his, she could have all of his attention on her. They were that combustible.

Whether Mr. Stoic-but-Sexy liked it or not—and she was going for not—it was what it was and what it was was flammable.

They reached her parking spot and Leah ignored his attempt to open her door. Instead, she placed her butt on the handle and crossed her ankles.

Seth's hand darted past her ear to grip the roof of her Jag. For a brief second the hair on his arms glinted in the passing lights of a car exiting the parking lot before they were plunged back into the shadows of the parking area. The street light on the other side of the lot didn't reach this part and she, reluctantly, admitted if she was alone, she might be a tiny bit nervous…but she was with Seth who would never let anything happen to her.

"Let's get going, Leah. It's late and standing around isn't smart."

"There are people, cars, going past all the time," Leah calmly replied.

She couldn't pretend she hadn't spoken those words in French, couldn't ignore the fact she'd told him, very graphically, that she wanted him in the most biblical way possible.

"I'm sorry if what I said earlier upset you," Leah said, her voice low.

Seth finally pulled his attention away from their surroundings and really looked at her. "Why would I be upset by what you said?"

"If I'd known that you spoke French, obviously I would've kept my mouth shut." Leah told him, staring at the tanned skin of his neck, the masculine vee at the bottom of his throat.

Seth's knuckle across her cheekbone was a soft as a butterfly's kiss. "Honey, I'm not upset. And, for your information, having a sexy woman lusting after me is a compliment and certainly nothing to be upset about."

Leah bit the corner of her bottom lip. She wanted to ask him how he felt, whether he was feeling the same but she'd rather chew her own wrists off before allowing herself to sound needy.

"Okay, then." She turned and tugged at the locked door handle. "No need to discuss that again." Leah pulled the handle again and frowned at Seth. "Will you please open the door?"

"Not just yet," Seth replied.

Leah threw her handsup in the air. "It's dark, it's dangerous, you want to get going."

Seth placed his hands on the side panels of the door on either side of Leah's hips. "As you said, we'll be fine for five minutes."

"But—"

Seth's mouth covered hers and when her mouth opened in surprise, his tongue slipped inside to touch hers and her brain switched off. There was just Seth and his clever mouth, one hand on her butt pushing her stomach into his erection, his other hand sliding up her rib cage before skimming his knuckles over her breast, rubbing her nipple in a move that sent heat and moisture between her thighs. Leah wiggled and Seth shoved his thigh between her legs, pushing her dress up her thigh so his knee could push into the thin fabric of her panties. Leah groaned into his mouth and wound her arms around his neck, wanting to slide inside him, needing heat on heat, skin on skin.

Needing more, she dropped her arms and shoved her hands up and under his loose shirt, looking for skin and finding his rock hard abs. Unable to stop, she allowed her fingers to dance over his hard erection, swallowing Seth's moan.

Oh, yeah, he wanted her as much as she wanted him. Leah moved her hands to his belt buckle, needing to have her fingers on him, to feel him between her palms, hot and hard and ready.

Seth slapped his hand on hers to keep her still and she pulled back from him, not understanding why they were stopping. She wanted him, he wanted her...what was the problem?

Seth held her wrists at her side and rested his forehead against hers. "We'll get arrested for public indecency."

Leah heard the sound of a car passing, laughter, footsteps. God, they were standing in the middle of a busy carport and Seth had just kissed her and she'd lost track of time and space. This wasn't good, this was so, so, not good.

"This is crazy," Leah whispered.

"Tell me about it," Seth replied.

"God, all I've done tonight is embarrass myself." Leah pulled her wrist from his grip to push her hair out of her eyes. "Sorry. Again. I'll stop throwing myself at you."

Seth's harsh sigh dropped into the warm air. "Nothing to apologize for," Seth muttered, stepping away from her. "And I was the one who started that kiss."

God, did he have to sound so together, so unaffected? So cool and in control?

"Leah, you are old enough to know that you and I have hectic chemistry and that it looks like we will, at some point, end up in bed." Seth's eyes gleamed in the low light. "I don't think either of us is strong enough to resist. So, yeah, at some point we are going to end up in bed. Or up against a wall or on the nearest horizontal surface."

"At some point?' Leah asked. That didn't sound like tonight...Dammit.

"At some point, probably not soon."

Well, hell.

Seth pushed his hand through his hair and shoved his hands into the pockets on his jeans, hunching his shoulders as he looked around. "I'm really uncomfortable standing out here, having this conversation with you out in the open. Can we go home and continue this discussion there?"

Leah narrowed her eyes. She gestured to a group of people approaching them from a distance. "Lots of people around, we're fine. Explain why us sleeping together isn't going to happen soon."

Seth glanced at his watch. "Two weeks and six days ago your life got flipped upside down. In the space of six hours you got married, were cheated on, and were arrested. All your dreams and plans came crashing down around your head. You feel betrayed and angry and hurt and all those messy emotions that normal people feel. I've wanted you since you walked into Jed and Mac's engagement party wearing a fire engine red top, denim shorts and fuck-me shoes."

He sounded like he was ordering breakfast, like them discussing sleeping together was the most normal thing in the world. It wasn't normal, not in her world. Couldn't he sound a little flustered, a wee bit out of his depth? It would make her feel less gauche, not so inexperienced and naïve.

"Why didn't you say something?"

Seth gave her a what-the-hell look. "Oh, maybe because you were engaged to be married! And because you're Jed's sister."

Oh, right. Fair point. "Well, I'm still Jed's sister and my marriage never started." Leah frowned. "Does it worry you that I'm still legally married?"

"It doesn't excite me but I know that it's over. I know exactly what happened, I was there when it happened." Seth sent her a steady look. "It's all going a bit fast, don't you think? I've only been here for three days. For both our sakes, let's try and slow this down, okay?"

Three days? That wasn't possible. "No way. You arrived on...Tuesday."

Seth smiled. "And today is Friday. Three days."

Leah groaned. "I'm losing my mind."

Seth pulled the passenger door open and gestured her inside. He sent her a grim smile. He looked down at her and muttered a phrase which she knew was Spanish. She understood "loca" and "pasión" but little else.

When Seth settled himself behind the wheel, she demanded to know what he said.

He grinned as he started the engine and flicked on the headlights. "Yeah, no. Learn Spanish."

★ ★ ★

SETH HEARD THE alert sound on his phone and he was instantly awake and groping for his phone. It took him a moment to make sense of what his screen was telling him: Leah's phone was more than two hundred yards from his and that it was on the move.

Seth cursed, immediately grasping that Leah was on the move with it.

Seth threw back the covers and looked at the face of his watch, grimacing when the luminous hands told him that it was just past two in the morning. He'd been living across the hall from Leah for not even a week and this late night alert was the first odd occurrence since they'd found that mannequin in the pool. He was no closer to finding the mystery person claiming to be his father and Fayed Khan was still in the wind. This wasn't the way he liked his operations to go. It was still early days, something would break soon. It had to.

Walking across the passage, he opened Leah's door and her empty bed confirmed what he knew to be true. Somehow and somewhat impressively, Leah had snuck out of the house. Seth stepped back into his room and looked longingly at his empty bed. Yanking his jeans off the back of a wingback chair, he dragged them on, pulled on a pair of socks and his tennis shoes. Shoving his hands into his hair, he pushed it back and ran his tongue over his teeth while he pulled on a t-shirt. Deciding he could take thirty seconds to brush his teeth, he ducked into the bathroom and took care of that.

He ran down the stairs, his eyes on the screen of his mobile. He'd placed the tracking devices on her phone and on her car the morning after the mannequin incident and he was grateful for his suspicious and mistrustful nature. Only the tracking device in her cell phone was activated, which meant she wasn't in her Jag. If she was, then there would be two dots on his screen. No, the Jag was still in the garage, which suggested Leah was either in a taxi, in a friend's car, or she'd been abducted from her own bed. He could, just and very reluctantly, swallow the possibility of Leah sneaking past him but he doubted that she could be taken without him knowing.

And that suggested she left the house under her own steam.

They would, be having words about that. Loud words, possibly angry words.*Lots* of words.

Seth jogged into the night and called her, impatient for her to answer. He could imagine her staring at the phone, debating whether to answer his call or not but eventually, and thank God, she did.

"What the hell are you up to?' he demanded, not bothering with niceties.

"Look, this is nothing. I didn't want to disturb you."

"You sneaking out of the house in the middle of the night is not nothing!" Seth yanked open the door to his rented SUV, climbed inside, and gunned the engine. "Where are you?"

"In a taxi heading toward the Sea Point area," Leah muttered.

"I'm sorry. I thought you said the Sea Point area. You know, where the hookers and drug dealers hang out?" Seth snapped, speeding through the gate as his mobile connected to the car's onboard computer. He dropped his phone into its holder before pulling his seat belt over his chest.

"How do you know that? You haven't been in the country long enough to know where the red light district is!" He heard the frustration in Leah's voice.

"I do my research," Seth said, gritting his teeth. "So tell me, are you freaking nuts?"

"Obviously I wouldn't be going to Sea Point if it wasn't important. Do you think I'm stupid?"

"Right now? Hell, yes, I think you're stupid!" Driving with one hand, Seth plugged "Sea Point" into his GPS and glared at the screen on his phone.

"Why?" Seth said after a ten second silence.

"Milo is in that area. He sent me a text message. He's drunk and he needs me to drive his car home. It's expensive and he doesn't want to leave it in the area."

Seth swore and shook his head. "And what the hell is he doing down there?"

Leah's sigh was audible over the phone. "Milo is…Milo has some… God, how do I put this? He has some sexual...leanings." Seth just waited her out and her next words flew out in a rush. "There are these fantasy, pop-up sex clubs where singles, couples, gay straight people go and have sex with whoever they fancy."

"They don't normally pop up in a bad part of town. They are usually in upmarket places, homes, suburbs," Seth said.

"Milo says that, sometimes, slumming it is part of the attraction. You don't seem shocked." Leah stated, her voice quiet.

He wasn't. Not yet.

"Kids involved?" Seth demanded.

"No! Fully consenting adults, or so Milo says."

Seth needed to keep her on the line, needed to have that connection as he whipped down side roads and across intersections to get to her. "I once tracked down the wild daughter of a scion of American politics who disappeared, willingly, into the sex world. I followed her and as a result I've seen some things that turned my stomach. Provided that there are no kids and no one is being forced to provide a service, I'm a live and let live type of guy. And after what I witnessed, you'd have to come up with a something very new and exceptionally weird to shock me."

"It still shocks me," Leah admitted. "I'm a bit weirded out by the concept."

"So, what's the plan? Are you going to go into this club and scoop him up?" Seth demanded, noticing that he was now only five minutes behind her.

"Pretty much," Leah said, her tone glum. "I might have

to bleach my eyes afterward."

"You have the brains God gave a gnat. And while I don't have a problem with how Milo gets his sexual kicks, I do have a problem with him phoning you to rescue him from a shitty part of town late at night," Seth muttered, ducking around a slow moving truck. "Right, Leah, listen up. When you get to the club, you stay in the taxi and wait for me to come and get you. You do not open the door for anyone but me."

Seth heard Leah convey his message to the driver and heard him say he wanted to get out of there as soon as possible.

"Tell him I'll pay him double." Seth interjected and heard the driver's agreement. As he thought, money had a way of getting him what he wanted. "You wait in the taxi, I'll come and get you and when you leave the taxi you stay right next to me, on my left side at all times."

"Why?"

Civilians, Seth did an eye roll. "I shoot with my right hand." Seth was quiet for a long time before releasing a deep, frustrated sigh. "Right now, I'm not sure whether I want to strangle you and tell you that you're incredibly stupid or to commend your obvious commitment to your friend."

"We're parked outside the club."

One minute. She was just around the corner. When he finally turned the corner, he saw the battered taxi and Leah's dark head inside and some tension drained from his shoulders. He pulled in behind the taxi and she turned and gave him a small smile. Seth frowned at her, holding her eyes but still speaking to her via his phone.

"I'd just like to state, for the record, that if you ever do something so categorically stupid again, you will not be able to sit down for a week. Are we clear?"

LEAH PEERED UP at the decayed buildings, yellow and spooky in the sodium light of the street lights. The flickering neon sign from the corner bar tossed green ribbons onto the pavement and momentarily turned the faces of the people milling outside the bar, bottles of beer in hand, into aliens.

Leah tried not to notice that the presence of a big, black expensive SUV caught their attention and more than a few heads lifted, obviously scenting an opportunity to do some illegal shopping.

Okay, admittedly, this wasn't the best idea she'd ever had. After escorting her out of the taxi, Seth climbed back behind the wheel of his SUV, his eyes constantly on the lookout for trouble.

Seth nodded to the phone in her hand. "Call Milo. Tell him to get his ass out here. We're not getting out the car until we see him. In fact, you're not getting out the car at all."

Leah lifted shaky hands and dialed and cursed when Milo's phone went straight to voice mail. Frowning at her answer, she disconnected and looked at Seth.

"It's still not going through," Leah said.

"Five minutes and we're out of here." Seth told her.

Dammit, Milo? Where are you? Leah tried to call him again and then heard the beep indicating that she'd received a text message.

"He left the club and he's in the lobby of the apartment block next door. He's drunk and needs my help."

"Yet he can send readable text messages? I don't like this. Something's off," Seth said. "Enough, we're gone."

Leah slapped her hand on his arm. "I can't just leave him, Seth! I have to check!"

Seth dropped a series of F-bombs that bounced around the interior of the car. He eventually nodded his agreement. "I can't leave you in the car alone so we stick together. Do not get out of the car until I open it. When you do, stay behind me."

Leah watched him walk around the hood, big and dangerous with his forbidding face and dark clothing. He stopped for a moment to watch the crowd on the pavement, who were watching them, his body quivering with tension. Leah scrambled out of the car when he opened the door and he immediately jerked her to his left side, placing his big body between her and the revelers.

"Move!" Seth hustled her towards the building and banged open the flimsy front door.

Pushing her inside, he looked around the empty lobby and Leah swallowed when she noticed his right hand ended in a lethal-looking pistol that he kept against his leg.

"See him?"

"No." Leah gestured to a dim passage way.

Seth stood at the entrance and frowned into the gloom.

"Stay where I can see you. You have a minute. If I don't see him, in that time, we're out of here."

Leah nodded and hurried down the passageway, stopping when she hit the corner. She called for Milo, keeping her voice low so she didn't wake any of the flat's inhabitants. When Milo didn't appear, Leah turned to Seth and lifted her hands in confusion.

"He had his chance. We're out of here." Seth latched his hand around her right wrist and yanked her towards the door. Holding her to the side of the door, he looked out onto the street and groaned.

Leah tried to look over his shoulder. "What's the problem?"

Seth peered up the street again. "Most of the onlookers have gone back inside."

"And why is that a bad thing?"

"If you're not an eyewitness, you can't give statements, especially if robbery turns to assault."

The blood drained from Leah's face. "Let's go back to the car," she said, grabbing his shirt in her clenched fist.

"I can see two, there'll be a third. They're waiting for us. Tats, tight clothing, knives. Good odds."

He sounded like he was ordering coffee. "Can't you just point your gun at them and tell them to get out of your way?"

"I'd prefer to keep guns out of the equation. No, quick and quiet."

Leah tried not to panic, tried to think, but she felt like a quivering mass of jelly.

Seth pressed the car keys into her hands. "When I say run, you fly to the car and get the hell out of here. I'll see you back at the house."

Seth didn't give her a chance to argue. The next minute was a blur of motion. Seth bulleted from the front door in a low, weaving run and slammed into the closest gang member. Leah heard the crack of an elbow against a head and saw Seth's booted foot fly out and connect with the chin of a knife-wielding lout who'd come to his friend's aid. Leah heard Seth's yell and flew down the path to the street as another gangster jumped Seth from behind.

The fight was a blur of motion…kick, punch, kick from both parties…and out of the corner of her eye she saw a body fly through the air and land across a metal dumpster. Horrified, she stood by the car, trembling with fear. Fear then turned to terror as a thick forearm crushed her windpipe and she felt herself being dragged away from the car across the tarmac.

Scratching her captor's arm with her fingernails, she twisted against his wiry body and wanted to gag at his sour breath on her cheek. Seth was still fighting off a fourth gang member on the other side of the car and she caught the glint of a wicked blade in the low light.

The bad guys had knives…

Then a whirling dervish vaulted across the hood of a car in a blur of speed, motion, and deadly intent. The sound of crushing bone and a pain saturated grunt accompanied the disappearance of the arm around her neck and she staggered backwards as Seth kicked a knife out of the hand of her assailant and followed the movement with a lightning fast kick to his temple.

"Where are the keys?" Seth yelled.

Leah looked down at her closed fist. Her white fingers were still wrapped around the set of keys. Seth pulled her fingers open, opened the door to his SUV and tossed her across to the passenger seat. She had barely settled her backside in the seat when he gunned the engine and accelerated away.

When they were on the freeway and heading for home, Seth took his foot off the accelerator and looked at Leah, huddled and shaking in the corner.

Seth dabbed his nostril with the back of his hand and winced when he saw blood on his hand. "You, angel, should come with a health warning."

Chapter Six

SETH CHECKED HIS rearview mirror and, wanting to put as much distance between them and the Sea Point area, veered in and out of the sparse traffic as fast as he possibly could. He risked a look at Leah's face and sighed when he saw that she was colorless. While she'd had grown up with strong, healthy, alpha males who were intimately acquainted with war, weapons, and hand to hand combat, he was convinced she'd never seen either her father or brother, or any man, in full warrior mode. Violence, for her, happened in action movies and on TV. Actually, that wasn't a bad analogy. In fact, the past hour felt exactly like he'd been acting in a B-grade action flick.

The world flashed by as Seth pushed the SUV through the central business district, heading for the motorway out of the city. Seth, intimately acquainted with adrenalin and far better able to deal with it, knew what she was feeling. She would be thinking the buildings were flying past the car and time had slowed down. Her mind would be floating, yet she felt like she could take on the world single-handed.

A car drifted into their lane and Leah nearly jumped out of her skin when she heard his low, inventive, stream of profanity directed at the driver as he ducked around the car to avoid a collision. He was sore, tired, and he also had to deal with idiotic drivers? In what universe was that fair?

What if one of those knives connected with her skin? What if he'd lost her, what if something had happened to her? Nothing scared him but, hell, losing her did.

Leah, knocking the side of her head with the base of her hand, distracted him from the terrifying road his mind was flying down.

"I feel funny," Leah said in a thin voice.

"Adrenalin." Seth snapped back, swinging onto the highway. "It happens when you get caught in stupid situations."

"This wasn't my fault. How was I expected to know that we'd be attacked by a gang?"

"Maybe the fact that it was a rough part of town and it's three o'clock in the bloody morning!" Seth roared. "You have the brains God gave a flea. You insisted on going into that building, wouldn't listen to me when I told you that I didn't like the situation! Didn't get in the freaking car like I told you to! And we still don't know where Milo is!"

"I know that and yelling at me won't help! And, by the way, I'm not one of your soldiers who you can boss around at will!"

"If you worked for me, you wouldn't last five minutes!" Seth slapped his hands on the steering wheel.

"That's because I'm a normal human being and not a fighting machine!"

"Normal? You? That's like calling C4 a cracker!"

"Screw you!" Leah's words lacked heat and power and

she lifted her hand to rub her throat.

Seth frowned as he noticed her hands patting the door handle, looking for the button to open the electric windows. He cracked the window for her and Leah lifted her face to the air. Seth powered around a bend, moved into the fast lane to pass a truck, and looked sideways. Sweat beads dotted Leah's forehead and her breathing was very shallow. Seth's hand on her shoulder pulled her back to her seat and he flicked another glance at her face. Shit! She was porcelain white and she was patting her throat.

"Leah?" He shook her shoulder and looked for an exit.

Leah didn't respond and Seth cursed. He lifted his hand and tapped her cheek with his finger, trying to get her to look at him.

"You're having a panic attack, Leah. You need to calm down. Just breathe." Seth kept his voice low, knowing his low but stern tone would pierce the fog threatening to consume her. "I'm pulling off, there's a gas station just ahead. You're safe. I'd never let anything happen to you. Breathe in for two and out for two, that's it."

"Don't…go."

"I'm not going anywhere. Just breathe, dammit!" Seth saw the bright lights of the gas station, pulled in, and whipped into a parking bay.

Slamming on the brakes, he left the car idling as he yanked his t-shirt off his head and doused it with water from the bottle he kept in the cup holder. Leaning across the seat, he wiped her fire-hot skin. By the expressions crossing her face, he understood there were a whole bunch of unpleasant images flashing in her head.

"Deeply, through your nose, in and out." Seth ordered and turned his t-shirt over and swiped the cool cloth down her neck and over her chest.

It was helping, because her breathing eventually settled and color seeped back into her face. Her eyes opened, met his, and he saw mortification under the naked fear.

"I think I had a panic attack," she mumbled.

The corners of Seth's mouth lifted. "I *know* you had a panic attack. The adrenalin faded and you bottomed out." Seth picked a strand of wet hair off her forehead and tucked it behind her ear. Seth doused his shirt with water again, wrung it out, and passed it to Leah when he resumed his position behind the wheel. "I wet it again. Drape it around your neck to keep you cool."

"Thanks, it helped. Seth, I—"

"We'll talk about it in the morning. No, Leah," he said when she opened her mouth to argue, "in the morning."

He knew she had the strength of a day-old kitten and he wasn't feeling that strong either. His body was starting to protest and he could feel where their attackers had got some solid blows in. He'd be sporting more than a couple of bruises in the morning.

Oh, well. He shrugged. At least he managed to do some damage in return—one would be singing soprano and another would have a hell of a headache—and he'd avoided their knives.

He'd rather be on the wrong side of a fist or a boot than a knife. The pointy ends tended to hurt.

★ ★ ★

"HAVE YOU HEARD from Milo?"

Leah walked down the stairs very early the next morning and shook her head at Seth's question. He was sitting on the bottom stair, lacing up his sneakers. They'd had less than three hours sleep but, unlike her, Seth looked as if he'd had a solid eight.

"I called or messaged him every twenty minutes since we got home last night and I haven't heard a thing." Leah bit her bottom lip. "I'm worried."

"He's not in the guest house. He didn't spend the night there." Seth told her, putting his hands on his hips.

Leah frowned. "How did you get into the guesthouse? I have the spare key..." She rolled her eyes. "Sorry, stupid question, I forgot who I was talking to."

"I have skills." Seth shrugged.

"Illegal skills."

"They come in handy."

"I'm going to kill him, Seth, seriously." Leah rubbed her hands over her face. She glanced down at the phone in her hand and blew out a long breath.

"He'll turn up."

Leah's phone vibrated and before the ring tone had time to kick in, she answered the call. "Where the hell have you been? I've been out of my mind worrying about you!"

"Wait...what?" Milo asked.

"Are you okay?' Leah demanded.

"I'm fine...what is the problem?" Milo asked. "Why are

you mad at me?"

Leah dropped the phone, looked at the screen in disbelief, and lifted it to her ear again. "Seth and I drove to Sea Point last night to pick you up—"

"What? Why?"

"You don't even remember? Milo, jeez! You were drunk and we couldn't find you. Oh, and did I mention that Seth had to fight off some gangbangers after we looked in that building for you?" Leah raised her voice, her temper rising.

"I wasn't in Sea Point last night—"

"Look, I don't have a problem with what you do and your…let's call them interests, but it wasn't fair for you to text me to come down to that area to pick you up. It was dangerous, Mi!"

"I didn't text you!"

"And I won't do it again—" Leah stopped and looked at Seth, her eyes wide with shock. "What did you say?"

"I wasn't in Sea Point and I didn't text you, call you, or send you a damned smoke signal." Milo said, his voice calm but irritated.

"But your name came up on my phone." Leah gabbled, her fingernails digging into Seth's skin. "The text came from your phone."

"Wasn't me, Lee. I spent the night at Jo's."

"Hold on a sec." Leah dropped her phone and looked at Seth. "He says it wasn't him, he spent the night meditating at a place called Jo's Cave. He probably has about ten people who can vouch for him."

Seth shook his head, looking disgusted. "His phone was

spoofed. The caller deliberately falsified the information transmitted into your display to disguise their identity. He knew you'd respond to Milo's text. That's why you couldn't reach him by phone last night." Seth took her cell from her hand, told Milo they'd get back to him, and disconnected the call.

He passed her phone back and tucked his hands under his armpits, thinking. After a couple of minutes, he lifted his head and his green eyes drilled into hers.

"Someone is messing with you, us. He lured us there and I suspect those gang members knew that we were coming, that they were paid to attack us. Shit."

"What?"

"It's a working theory, one I need to think about. I think best when I run. Why don't you come for a run with me? We'll work off some tension on the road." Seth suggested and Leah nodded.

She ran up to her room, quickly changed into shorts and a sports bra, and jogged back down the stairs.

Since Seth was deep in thought and didn't seem inclined to talk, they warmed up in silence and then left the property via a side gate, opening it with the remote device that Seth then tucked into the pocket of his basketball shorts. Leah noticed he shortened his stride to allow her to keep an easy pace and she followed his lead when he angled off so that they could run on the promenade that ran along the beach-front.

It was a brilliant summer's morning, the kind of morning when she was happy to be up early; cool enough to run in comfort but knowing that the temperature would climb later in the day. A lazy sea kissed the clean beaches and a few die-hard surfers tried to coax rides off two foot waves. A few fellow joggers shared the space with them and Leah let the occasional snippets of conservation wash over her as she allowed her stride to lengthen and her muscles to relax. Seth immediately sensed her need to push herself and picked up his pace, as if he were silently urging her to keep up. Leah felt her heart rate kick as they dodged past the slower joggers and found a stretch of open pavement. Every kilometer or so, Seth increased their speed and she eventually lifted her hand call uncle, to tell him she was at her limit. She knew he had a lot more in reserve but felt grateful when he slowed his pace to a steady jog and then to a walk.

Leah put her hands on her knees and sucked in air. When she felt like she could string a coherent sentence together, she lifted her head. "I needed that."

Seth rested his broad palm on her back for a moment. "I know. I did, too. But we need to keep walking or else we're going to stiffen up."

Leah fell into step beside him, her hands on her hips.

"Want some water and a cup of coffee?" Seth nodded to a food truck advertising both a little way from them.

At her nod, Seth walked away and Leah moved to the low wall and did some stretches to cool down. She smiled as a plump jogger caught sight of Seth and her jaw fell to the ground. Leah smiled as the woman's friend yanked her out of the way of an oncoming cyclist. Leah sympathized; Seth had the same effect on her.

Seth returned, placed their coffee on the wall and cracked the seal on the water bottle before handing it over. Leah drank half the bottle and reached for her coffee. Sitting cross legged on the wall, she lifted the lid of her cup and inhaled deeply.

Seth joined her on the wall and stretched his long legs out in front of him.

Seth sipped and rolled his head from side to side. "I left you at your door last night but when I came down, I found you asleep on the couch in front of the TV."

Leah's fingers tightened on her coffee cup. "Yeah, I couldn't sleep so I came down to watch some television."

"You have a TV in your room, why not watch it there?"

He was as sharp as those knives that were pointed in his direction last night. Leah looked for an explanation but decided that she was just too tired to come up with one that sounded plausible. So she went with the truth. "I haven't managed to sleep in a bed since that night we spent in jail."

A small frown appeared between Seth's dark eyebrows. "Why not?"

Leah lifted one shoulder and quickly dropped it again. "I try, most nights but I close my eyes and I see Heath and Sara in my wedding bed…stupid, I know. It's not like I love him anymore."

"Did you ever?" Seth asked.

"I was going to marry him, Seth." It was all she could think of to say.

"A lot of people marry for reasons other than love. Or are conned into believing they're in love. Few marry knowing that this is absolutely, one hundred and fifty percent, what they want to do," Seth said, in his ordering breakfast voice. "So, did you really, really love him?"

She wanted to tell him she had, that marrying Heath was what she really wanted to do, but Seth would call her on her lie. "I wanted to be married, I wanted kids. I probably wanted those more than I wanted Heath."

Seth crossed his ankles and crumpled his empty coffee cup. "We've got to get you back to sleeping in your bed."

Leah cocked her head and her mouth twitched at the flirty mischief in Seth's eyes. "And what do you propose, Mr. Halcott? Are you offering to chase those ghosts out of my bed?"

Seth grinned. "Not yet. But we are closer to that happening."

Leah groaned. "You're killing me, Halcott."

"Talking about murder, you do know Jed is going to kill me, don't you?" Seth asked her, his voice dropping and become serious. "If we have an affair and Jed finds out, he will take me apart."

"I'm an adult, Seth, and I am perfectly able to make my own decisions about who I allow into my bed."

"Sure, but you're also Jed's baby sister and your being adult is not going to stop him from going ballistic." Seth stared down at the coffee in his hand. "It could hurt our friendship, Leah."

Dammit, she hadn't thought about that. "And that worries you?"

"Damn straight that worries me. I don't have that many

friends that I can play fast and loose with the ones that I have. I'm risking our friendship for..."

"For sex, with me," Leah said and she regretted the bitterness she heard in her tone.

She had no right to be hurt, to feel rejected, Jed and Seth's friendship was a long-standing one, built on bullets and bombs and trust. Seth had a right to protect his friendship—even though Jed had no right to be upset about her and Seth—and it was the honorable thing to do. It was even the right thing to do. How could she compete? She shouldn't feel hurt. She had no right to be hurt. But she couldn't help feeling that she was, again, second best, someone's second choice. *But it's only sex. You have no right to be upset about this.* If sex was all she wanted then she could go to a bar or club and she was sure she could find someone with whom she could have some fun with.

Fun...that was what she was after, wasn't it? Honesty compelled her to admit, even without any sex, she enjoyed spending time with Seth, being with Seth. She liked his sharp brain, his slightly acerbic tongue, his confidence. But liking Seth, beyond the physical, was dangerous.

Leah sighed and blew air into her cheeks. This wasn't supposed to be so complicated. Sex, a little bedroom-based fun and they'd both move on. But her farcical marriage, her stupid husband-in-name-only and whoever it was who was playing games with them was standing between her and Seth and a little, or a lot, of fun.

It would be easier if they just stopped this, put the brakes on, stopped thinking about sleeping together. It would be simpler, cut and dried...When life kept throwing up roadblocks maybe it was time to reevaluate and heed the warning signs.

Leah felt Seth's hand under her chin, turning her head and then he dragged his lips over hers, as if he were desperate to taste her again. Caught off guard, she noticed he closed his eyes and she felt his small sigh on her lips. Her hand curled around his hard neck and he echoed her action by digging his fingers into her hip. His thumb found the bare strip of skin above her jogging shorts and he dusted sparks across her skin with every swipe. His mouth curved into a smile over hers and just like that, thoughts of Jed and Heath and the ugliness of last night faded away. Milo was fine, grumpy but unhurt, the sun was shining, and Seth was kissing her, his tongue slow dancing with hers. Life, right now, at this moment, was good.

How was she supposed to back away from him when he kissed like a dream, kissed like he was created to kiss her? How could she resist him, how could she walk away from this heat? If she did, he would be her biggest regret and she'd always be disappointed she'd never experienced what making love with him felt like.

"Your brain is spinning," Seth muttered against her lips.

"Yeah," Leah whispered back.

"About?"

Leah gathered her courage. "That maybe it would be better if we didn't...you know."

"Make love?" Seth clarified, their breaths still mingling. Seth pulled his head back, looking rueful. "Honey, neither of us is that smart. It's going to happen, maybe not today, or tomorrow, but at some point. And we're just going to have to live with the consequences."

Seth stood up and pulled her to her feet. "Come on, let's get going. I'd like to swing past the Khan's house before you head in to work."

★ ★ ★

HE DIDN'T THINK that he could resist her for much longer. Seth stood in the kitchen waiting for Leah to come downstairs. He'd only been in Cape Town for just six days but he felt like he'd been waiting for Leah forever. Their attraction kept burning bigger and brighter and, to be honest, it scared him. This didn't happen in real life, normal life. He was a guy who'd had a lot of sex over a lot of years, and whatever the hell was happening between him and Leah was atypical. In his experience, situations that built so quickly, usually died even faster.

Usually by detonation.

The attraction he could handle—Leah was a sexy woman—but he was disconcerted by the fact that he liked Leah more than he expected to, that he was as attracted to her mind as well as her body. And, if he were being very honest, that mental attraction was the reason he was applying pressure to the brakes. He could easily sleep with her and leave if he wasn't mentally…intrigued, but leaving would not come as easy if she managed to slip under his skin. Commitment, a steady relationship, wasn't his thing, he was a rolling stone, a nomad, he gave everything he had to his job and then another hundred percent into tracking down The Recruiter.

He couldn't afford to feel more for her than he should. He had a job, a life back in New York, hers was here. She was three weeks off a crazy breakup situation, still vulnerable and oh, yeah, she was still married, dammit!

And, the other little thing, they had some asshole playing dangerous games with them and he had a missing teenager to find.

Sleeping with Leah, losing himself in Leah, was a distraction he could not afford. *Sort your priorities out, dumbass.*

Seth picked up his flashing phone and saw a message from his Pytheon contact, saying he had no news on his fake father but it might be worthwhile for Sethto talk to a young man called Abdullah Ali, the leader of a small group connected to Fayed's mosque embracing radical viewpoints. He might, or might not, know Fayed. Some US dollars would help him remember.

Funny how, all over the world, dollars had the magical ability to restore memory.

"Problem?" Leah asked.

Seth looked at her and shook his head. "No, maybe a lead on Fayed." Seth looked down at his phone again. "And my colleague landed this morning; he's supposed to help me with both situations."

Leah made him a cup of coffee and Seth lifted the mug to his lips and took a sip of the scalding liquid.

Leah's eyes radiated sympathy. "God, the Khan's must be

mad with worry." She dumped more sugar into her coffee and looked thoughtful as she stirred the liquid. "Do you have any ideas on where he went? And how to get him back?"

Seth wished he did. "Nothing at the moment, which isn't unusual. We suspect we know who took him but trying to track him is like trying to catch mist. The guy is a freakin' ghost. Hopefully my contact's lead will point me in the right direction."

"Kids talk, especially teenagers. They can't keep their mouths closed. I'd bet any money that one of the kid's friends know where he is or where he's gone."

"I was thinking the same thing. I'll send Jett to talk to them; maybe he'll get something out of them."

Seth noticed Leah was tapping her finger against her mug, a sign that she was about to say something. She nibbled the inside of her cheek and he waited patiently.

"About last night…" Leah started. She looked toward the kitchen window, sighed and wrinkled her nose. "I shouldn't have left, shouldn't have gone out on my own. I should've trusted you enough to ask for help."

"Why didn't you?" Seth asked, leaning back against the counter.

Leah shrugged. "It wasn't something I haven't done ten, twelve, fifteen, times before. Milo gets into situations and I go and get him. I thought last night would be more of the same. I didn't want to bother you with something that has never been an issue for me before."

"When was the last time you did that?" Seth asked, frowning.

"Rescue Milo? Um...actually, it was a couple of days after the wedding."

Seth thought for a minute and nodded. "Time line wise, I think that makes sense."

Leah frowned at him, obviously not following. "I'm not sure what you're getting at."

"I was here in Cape Town at your wedding nearly three weeks ago. I think my fake-father-slash-real-father got wind of that, I have no idea how. Through your wedding and your arrest he made the connection of you to me, via Jed. He was watching me then, here. It's a lot easier to do than in New York...yeah, that makes sense. He planned to bring me back here, planned to use you to get to me."

Leah swallowed. "So those thugs last night were supposed to kill us, kidnap us?"

Whatever plans were in place, they failed. But, yes, I think they had orders to take me out of the game. You were collateral damage."

Leah flinched and her color faded but she didn't drop her eyes from his. "I'm fairly glad that you are, as you said, hard to kill."

"Damn straight."

"But why?" Leah threw her hands up in the air. "What does he want?"

Seth wished he knew. But this was an elaborate plan, something that took time and thought and a lot of preparation. This was a guy with an agenda. Unfortunately he had, thanks to his position in Pytheon, a long list of people pissed at him. And the person at the top of that list was The Recruiter, the same guy who snatched Fayed from Cape

Town.

Too many coincidences. Coincidences made him itchy.

"Anyway, I just wanted to say sorry, that I put us in that stupid situation, that I put you in danger," Leah said, her eyes on his.

A simple apology, no frills, no excuses. Shit, Seth thought, another reason to like this fascinating woman.

"Accepted. Don't do it again." Seth couldn't help stepping forward, rubbing his thumb across her full bottom lip.

He wanted to kiss her but he didn't dare; he didn't think he'd stop at a kiss. So much heat and want and craziness. The air between them swayed and shimmered, thickened and danced. The hair on his arms lifted and he saw the shiver that skittered across her skin. And the shiver wasn't from cold…she wanted him as much as he wanted her.

He couldn't, he shouldn't. This was Leah, not a quick roll in the hay. She was someone he couldn't bag, tag, and toss away.

Seth watched as the tip of her pink tongue peeked out from between her teeth. Her gaze bounced from his eyes to his mouth and back up again. If he didn't step away right now, he would take her, right here, right on the floor.

It took everything he had to speak and not kiss her. "Next time, please, just trust me, okay?"

Leah nodded. "Okay. I promise to talk to you before I do anything stupid. I might still do it," she said with refreshing honesty, "but I'll talk to you about it first."

Seth had to smile. Yeah, he liked her a lot. Far, far more than he should.

Chapter Seven

FORTY FIVE MINUTES later, Seth turned onto the oak-lined road and idly listened to Leah talking on her phone. From what he could gather, she had the sole mandate on a very exclusive property in Camps Bay and she needed Milo to show a prospective buyer the property.

"They are a bit concerned that the property won't be big enough but the view will sell it. If they want to haggle over the price, let them. I've built in some wiggle room," Leah said.

She was a savvy business woman; he supposed she'd had to be to build up such a successful business before turning thirty. Leah was wearing a thigh-length swing dress in black and yellow and gray, obviously expensive, designer shoes, and her bag and sunglasses were high-end couture. Yeah, she had money but, unlike his previous girlfriends, Leah paid her own way.

Not that she was his girlfriend; that was just a figure of speech. *Stop looking at her legs, Halcott.* Slowing down, he approached the wrought iron gates of the Khan's property. A tall, gangly kid was walking along the sidewalk, he should be in school. The hair on the back of his head lifted.

He should be in school. Seth took a closer look at the face beneath the grey hoodie and gasped his surprise. Holy shit....Fayed?

No fucking way!

Seth watched, astonished as the teenager casually strode up to the intercom and placed his finger on the bell. He swung the car into the driveway and pushed the button to take his window down, his heart thundering in his chest. Fayed stood between the intercom and the car and it took all of Seth's willpower not to toss him into the car and roar up the drive.

"Fayed Khan?"

Out of the corner of his eyes he saw Leah's head shoot up and he heard her gasp. He ignored her and didn't take his eyes off the sulky looking teenager.

"Yeah. Who are you?"

"Seth Halcott. I've been looking for you."

Fayed lifted his shoulders in an insouciant shrug. "Well, you found me. Now piss off and leave me alone."

★ ★ ★

FAYED'S MOTHER WAS keening with joy, his sister was looking shocked, and his father looked like Seth could push him over with a fingertip. Their missing son was back and none of them seemed sure how to act or what to do.

The only Khan member not caught up with the drama was the kid himself, he just looked bored. And utterly miserable to be home.

"Weird," Leah said, nudging Seth, who stood next to

her, watching the family reunion.

"Fayed's reaction? Very weird indeed," Seth replied in a tone just low enough for her to hear.

Fatima Khan lifted her head from Fayed's shoulder, looked at him, and burst into tears again. Fayed rolled his eyes when his mother's arms squeezed him again and Leah resisted the urge to smack the annoyance off his face.

The kid definitely needed to be put back into his box.

"Okay, let's move this along," Seth said, still speaking in her ear. "Can you help me out by taking the women back to the kitchen and settling them down?"

"Yeah sure," Leah said, placing her hand on his arm. "What are you going to do?"

"Find out what the hell is going on here," Seth muttered. "This never happens, kids never just, literally, walk back into their families lives, not like this."

Leah's hand moved down his arm and she linked her fingers in his, quickly squeezing. "You'll get to the bottom of it, Seth."

Seth's thumb drifted across the ball of her hand as he looked at her. "Yeah, I will." He pulled in a deep breath and let go of her hand. "Let's do this."

Leah nodded, walked over to Fayed's mom and put a hand around her shoulder. "Mrs. Khan, come with me now. Let's get you calmed down."

Leah steered the teenager's mother and sister out of the hall. Looking back, she saw Seth place his hand on the back of Fayed's neck. "I think your son has some explaining to do, Mr. Khan."

Leah couldn't wait to hear the story he came up with.

★ ★ ★

SETH HAD BEEN expecting a call from the new Pytheon agent but he hadn't expected Jett to rock up on Leah's doorstep ten minutes after they'd returned to the house that evening. It had been a long day; he'd spent most of it talking to Fayed, trying to get the sullen kid to open up. Nothing he did or said cracked his shell; he'd told Seth all he intended to and then retreated into surly silence.

Right now, all he wanted to do was sit on the veranda with a cold beer and think. Actually, that wasn't what he most wanted to do but it was as good as he was going to get.

Seth opened the front door, gestured his newest agent into the hall and held out his hand and introduced himself.

"I thought I'd come by and meet you, get up to speed on the case." Jett stated, shoving a hand into his scruffy, black hair. He pulled his sunglasses off his face and tapped them against the palm of his hand.

"Yeah, the case that's been flipped on its head," Seth said.

Seth watched as Leah walked into the hall from the kitchen, carrying two beer bottles. They'd intended to drink them on the verandah, together, trying to wind down after an intense day. Seth sighed and admitted it was maybe a good thing that Jett was here. He wouldn't be tempted to relieve his stress in the time-honored, most fun way possible.

Seth quickly made introductions and narrowed his eyes

when Leah left her hand in Jett's a little too long. And maybe he was losing his mind if Leah's hand in Jett's annoyed him.

"Let's talk on the veranda." Seth suggested, wanting Jett to move along.

Jett's bright blue gaze stayed on Leah and he slowly raised an eyebrow. Seth eventually caught on… Jett thought that they needed privacy to talk freely.

"Leah knows the situation. We can talk in front of her."

Leah lifted a bottle and her eyebrow at Jett. "Want a beer?"

"Sure, thanks."

Leah handed the bottles over. "I'll get another for myself but, if you don't mind, I'm going to skip the conversation. I've got some work to do and Seth and I have already discussed what happened today."

"I won't take long, Miss Hamilton," Jet said and flashed a smile Seth knew could melt the elastic in lingerie at twenty paces.

Leah's face softened and he thought he saw the flutter of her eyelashes. God! It was too early in their relationship for his newest agent to piss him off.

"Eyes front, soldier," Seth muttered, in a tone so low that only Jett could hear.

Jett's sardonic look—his agents weren't big on kowtowing and he normally liked that—was followed by a knowing grin.

Legend or not, this guy was starting to annoy the shit out of Seth.

"Let's go." Seth ordered, whipping around and walking

through the lounge towards the doors that led to the veranda. Jett followed him out and immediately went to the railing and rested his forearms on the top rail and looked out over the tiny fishing harbor. Brightly colored boats were heading out to sea and the water looked like it couldn't decide whether it wanted to wear green or blue today.

"Nice view. Pretty city," Jett said.

It was but Seth didn't want to hear Jett's opinions on the scenery of the Western Cape.

"So, what did I miss today?" Jett asked.

Seth took a long sip of his beer and rested the cool bottle against his forehead. He took a seat on one of the outdoor chairs and gestured Jett to follow suit. When Jett sat down, Seth placed his bottle on the table separating them and placed his foot on his opposite knee.

"Weird day. Leah and I went to the Khan's house. She was busy on a call, I was driving. And I see this kid walking down the road. I think he looks familiar and he comes closer and I think, hell, no way. It's Fayed. He goes up to the gate and pushes the bell."

Jett frowned, looking like he wasn't sure he'd heard Seth right. "Fayed, the missing kid, walked up to the gate and pushed the bell?"

Seth nodded. "There he was, perfectly fine, acting like it was the most normal thing in the world to be missing for over a week and to return home like nothing had happened. I accompany the kid into the house and the family sees him and it's mayhem."

Jett raised his eyebrows and waited for Seth to continue.

"Leah takes charge of his mom and sister and I pull a very unhappy Fayed and his father into a study. As soon as I close the door, the father backhands the kid, his ring cuts his bottom lip." Seth winced, remembering. He understood how emotion bubbled over but that was a hell of a homecoming for any kid.

"The kid starts screaming at the father in Arabic which I understand. It turns out that Fayed didn't want to come back home, he said The Recruiter said that he wasn't fit to fight. That he wasn't dedicated enough, strong enough for jihad. The kid is big time pissed off."

Jett frowned. "What? Hold on, that doesn't make sense. The kid has hacking skills, he could be used, somewhere. And the only way kids normally return home is by ransom, escape, which is rare, or in a body bag. Extremist organizations aren't known for being picky about their recruits."

Exactly. Seth sat on the corner of the wooden table and looked past Jett to the horizon and the container ship that was the size of a matchbox.

"Can he identify where he's been for the past few days?" Jett asked.

"He says not. He was collected in an SUV type car, dark blue or black—" Seth stood up and walked up to the railing.

"Did he meet The Recruiter?"

Seth frowned. "He said he did."

Jett cocked his head, obviously picking up something in his tone. "Shouldn't he have?"

"The Recruiter always keeps his distance from his targets. So, if the kid saw The Recruiter, then that's a huge change in his MO." Seth explained. "And the bigger question is, if that's true, why? Why did he let this kid see him and why did he let him go?" Seth added. "And what game is he playing?"

Jett placed his designer sunglasses back onto his face and he looked like the big badass he was. "What do you want me to do?"

Seth thought for a moment. "Go back to the Khan house. Pump the kid for more information. Arrange for him to meet with a sketch artist, maybe we can get a composite drawing? Then—"

"I'll try to work out where he was kept, how he contacted The Recruiter, if he saw anyone else. I know the drill." Jett stated.

Seth speared his fingers into his hair. "Sorry, I don't normally micromanage."

"Good to know."

Seth jammed his hands into the pockets of his cream shorts and rocked on his heels. "I'm missing something, I know it. Something is off..."

"Good enough for me," Jett replied, standing up and stretching. "I'll keep digging."

Seth looked at him, bemused. "You strike me as the type who makes up his own mind, Smith-Jones, or is your take-me-at-my-word attitude your way of trying to impress me?"

"I'm not the type who plasters my tongue on my boss's ass."

Seth winced at his analogy.

"And I always make up my own mind. I just happen to

agree with you," Jett retorted, moving towards the doors leading to the lounge. "You have a rep for seeing patterns where there aren't any, seeing a picture that no one else can. If your gut is screaming there's something off with this situation then I'm going to listen."

Seth hated to admit it but he was humbled and touched that this hard ass, well-respected soldier trusted him and trusted his instincts. Yeah, Smith-Jones was going to be hell on wheels to manage but he sensed this man was going to do some amazing things. What, he wasn't sure, but he was looking forward to the fireworks.

"Check Fayed's story. Find me something." Seth barked out the order but he could tell Jett wasn't even remotely intimidated.

"Can I bend the rules?" Jett asked.

Seth couldn't help his small smile. "Don't get caught."

Oh yeah, fireworks.

★ ★ ★

WAS SHE REALLY eavesdropping if she stood in the hall of her own home and listened to the conversation in the guest room? Of course it was but she didn't care. Listening to Seth issue orders and run through scenarios was as sexy as hell even if she didn't know what he was talking about half the time. From the little she did understand, a missing student had been found in Beijing, an art museum was missing a lesser known French impressionistic painting and someone had been conned out of a rather nice cache of diamonds.

Leah walked down to the kitchen, poured herself a glass of juice, drank that, ate half a bowl of peanut butter ice cream, and when she returned a half hour later, Seth was still on his cell phone talking to someone called Stone. Leah looked through his half open door and saw Seth sitting at the desk in the corner, his bare back to her. His phone was tucked between his shoulder and neck and he was tapping the keyboard of his laptop.

"Tell Forsythe that I'll rip his head off if he does anything that stupid again." Seth said, his voice razor sharp. "No, don't bother, I'll call him now and rip him a new one. *Idiot.* He not only could've killed himself but blown a two-year op as well."

Seth ran his hand through his hair and rubbed the back of his neck. She wished she had the right to walk into his room and place her hands on his shoulders and massage the tension out of his muscles, drop her head to kiss the sexy dip where his muscle met his shoulder, taste the dimples on either side of his hip.

She wanted him. Leah turned away. She wanted him with a ferocity that terrified her. Leah sighed as she walked into her room. This was about more than sex. It was about a connection, respect, a lot of liking. It was about sharing herself with a good man, someone mentally and physically strong. She wanted his heat and touch but she also wanted his intense focus, the concentration he gave to work, on her. Tonight, she needed him, she needed *that.*

Yes, there were reasons why they shouldn't be together, good and valid reasons. They'd didn't know each other well, this was all moving too fast—super fast!—he was her brother's best friend, she was just out of an intense relationship….blah, blah, boring. When last was she brave enough to ask for what she wanted, courageous enough to express what she wanted?

She wasn't a rule breaker, she worked hard, was loyal, she tried to be a good sister, daughter, friend. But when last did she give herself permission to take something for herself, when last did she think of her and only her? She couldn't remember…

Tonight, she wanted to ditch the excuses, forget the complications, and live. Seize the moment.

There was a sexy, ripped man in her house who seemed to want her as much as she wanted him and, having survived a few shitty weeks, he would be her present to herself.

They'd deal with the consequences; they'd face the music, but not tonight.

Tonight they needed to step out of their lives, away from the madness, and live. And love. And feast. And Seth needed to escape as much as she did.

Not allowing herself time to think, knowing if she didn't act now, she'd talk herself out of it. Leah walked out of her room and slipped through his half-open door. He'd stopped working and was in the shower.

Naked Seth in the shower. Yum.

The bathroom door was almost closed making it so much easier to sneak.

"For God sake, Leah," Seth said and partially pulled back the shower curtain to scowl at her before disappearing behind the red curtain again. "Can what you want wait until I'm done?"

So much for sneaking.

Shaking with nerves or adrenalin, Leah wasn't sure which—what if he made her get dressed? What if he rejected her? Leah lifted her pajama vest over her head. When she dropped it to the floor, she looked up and Seth had the curtain pulled back and was looking at her like she'd lost her mind. Or that she had the most fantastic boobs ever.

"Shit, Leah," he muttered before whipping the curtain closed again.

Leah hooked her thumbs into her pajama bottoms and shimmied them down her hips, leaving her completely nude. She wasn't used to feeling so exposed. She and Heath had never been the most adventurous or even comfortable of lovers. *Courage, Hamilton.* She pulled the curtain back and allowed her eyes the sheer pleasure of travelling over his body. She'd seen his chest and six pack before so she skipped those and looked down to the thick hair at his groin and, more importantly, his rapidly expanding cock. It was thick and hard and it pulsed beneath her gaze and she wanted to wrap her hands around him, explore him, feel him pushing inside her, filling her.

When she reached his face, his strong mouth was twisted into a rueful smile and his eyes lightened to a special shade of green.

His thoughts couldn't have been clearer if he'd tattooed them on her skin. *Yeah, I think you're pretty hot, too.*

He was naked, she was naked and she was not leaving

here until her curiosity was satisfied. And she was plenty curious.

"Guess we're going to be doing this sooner rather than later," Seth said, oblivious to the water pounding his head, his back.

His face was all fierce resolve. Impatient, determined, and relentless. Seth reached for her and placed his hands on her hips and easily lifted her into the tub and pulled her so they stood hip to hip and chest to chest.

Seth slid his fingers into her hair above her ear. Tipping her face, Seth bent his head and kissed her. Thoroughly, completely, competently…his tongue slid into her mouth and she welcomed his heat, his passion, his desire for her evident in the groans he made in the back of his throat, his fingers clenching her hip.

Leah had doubted she could surrender so completely to a man again but she felt herself falling, sliding, deeper into him. Even with just his mouth on hers and his hand on her head and her hip, she knew she was, momentarily, under his control. She wound her arms around his waist and pushed into him, her hands exploring the skin covered muscles of his back.

"This is a onetime deal, Leah. It's all we can have." Seth broke their kiss, placing his hot, open mouth on her cheekbone. "One hit, then we get back to real life, go back to where we were."

Could they? With this much passion? She didn't think so.

"Better make it good then," Leah murmured.

"I intend to but I'd prefer that we take this to the bedroom."

Slipping his hands under Leah's thighs, he hauled her up and she locked her legs around his waist. His mouth nibbled her neck as he walked them back into the bedroom and sat down on the bed. Leah straddled his thighs and Seth cupped her face with his big hands. He pushed a strand of hair behind her ear and traced her mouth with a calloused thumb.

His eyes, when they met hers, were serious. "Are you sure you want to do this?"

Leah took his hand and placed it on her breast. "Just be with me. Feel me."

Seth's hands dropped to waist and slid over her back and butt, down her thighs and back up again. He teased her lips, her jaw, tugged her earlobe with his teeth. Still holding her, Seth stood up and turned around and gently lowered her down on the bed. He took a step back and, supremely unselfconscious about his own nudity, stared at her body. Then his eyes darkened, narrowed as he knelt on the bed next to her, his eyes drifting from her nipples, her belly button, the tiny triangle of hair at the juncture of her thighs. When she thought she couldn't stand another second of not having him touching her, Seth covered her breast with his hand and he bent his head to kiss her, his tongue sweeping into her mouth and flipping the switch that shut down her brain.

He was hard and big and she was lost in his taste and smell and masculinity. His hands stroked and smoothed, his voice reassured as it rumbled over her skin, his tongue probed, stroked, and swirled. At times she wasn't sure where she ended and he started, whether it was her moans or his she heard deep in her soul, whether she would ever feel this free, this uninhibited again. He encouraged and complimented as he pushed her higher and higher, causing her breath to fumble and her skin to heat. Hands and mouth caressed those long neglected places; the crook of her elbow, her belly button, the soft inside of her thigh.

Long luscious, breath-stealing moments passed and Leah found herself drifting or a ribbon of pure pleasure. So this was what good sex felt like. Leah softly protested when Seth pulled back from her and reached across her to dip his hand into the bedside drawer. He cursed and eventually pulled out a strip of condoms. After sliding his mouth across hers, he pulled a foil packet from the strip and quickly and efficiently sheathed himself with the latex.

Thank God one of them was thinking straight. Yeah, she was on the pill but she hadn't thought about protection at all.

Then Seth pulled a nipple into his mouth and all thoughts of protection evaporated. He was hot and hard and she was ready when he slid into her, taking them to a place that was faster, higher, crazier. He held back and teased, plunged and varied his rhythm as he drove her upwards. Leah heard his labored breath in her ear, his dirty commands and knew he was holding himself back, waiting for her to fly. Reaching for the little death, she crested, and fell, crested again and Seth rode that wave with her until he tensed, shouted, and spasmed within her.

Seth lifted himself up and off her, dropping a kiss on her stomach before flopping onto his back. He pulled her onto his chest, his broad hand running down her back in long strokes.

"Ggnnnh?" Seth pushed the sound through his lips.

Leah smiled up at him and his heart bumped. She scooted up his chest and laid her mouth on his.

"Ggnnnh?" Leah tried to imitate the sound he made.

"That was caveman for 'you blow my socks off'."

Leah lifted her head and looked down at his bare feet. "You're not wearing any socks."

"That's because you blew them off."

Leah wanted to giggle, thrilled at the idea she'd affected him as much as he did her. Leah kissed his chest, enjoying his rhythmic breathing, his soft hair under her hand, the hard muscles under masculine skin. Nothing had ever felt as insanely amazing as when he'd pushed into her; it was as if she'd been waiting for him for a long, long time.

Seth patted her butt and she pulled back to look at him and sighed at his serious face. "Something wrong?" she asked.

Okay, she knew he wasn't a cuddly type of guy, that this wasn't anything but a mutual pursuit of pleasure but five minutes ago she'd shattered in his arms. Couldn't he give her a little more time to recover?

"I'm expecting a call. I was taking a quick shower while I waited."

*Uh huh.*Leah rolled off him. That might be true but it was also a damn fine excuse to avoid the touchy-feely, cuddling part of the program.

"Sorry. I need to do this, it's important," Seth said, his voice extra rough.

Leah blinked away the burning sensation in her eyes. "Sure, I understand," Leah said, her voice conveying exactly the opposite.

Seth muttered a curse as he left the bed and walked back into the bathroom. When he returned, a towel around his waist, he placed a hand on her shoulder and she was surprised when he sat down next to her and dropped a kiss on her upper arm. "I need to work, honey."

Leah rolled over and frowned, not understanding. This was her house and her bedroom…oh, hell, she was in the spare bedroom and Seth obviously needed privacy to take his call.

Leah climbed out the side of the bed Seth wasn't on and, realizing her clothes were in his bathroom, whipped a t-shirt from the pile of laundry on top of a chest of drawers. She pulled it over her head as his computer buzzed with an incoming call. She glared at the screen and pulled her hair out from the collar of the t-shirt.

She couldn't whine, she couldn't complain, she'd come here and she'd received exactly what she'd wanted. Her only course of action was to leave the room with as much dignity as possible.

She walked around and gestured to the bed. "Thanks. As I said, it was fun."

Seth looked at his computer and rubbed the back of his neck. "I'll try and wrap this up—"

Leah lifted her hands and managed to pull a smile onto her face. "It's okay, seriously. I'll let you work."

Leah walked out of the room, pulling the door closed behind her. She blew out a long breath and stumbled across the empty hall to her own bedroom. She locked the door behind her and sat on the edge of her bed.

So, ignoring the way it ended, making love with Seth had been—cliché time—magical and it made the quick fumbles she'd shared with Heath seem childish and silly. She'd never known the depth of physical satisfaction she was capable of until Seth put his clever hands and mobile mouth on her body. And she'd responded with some moves that she didn't know she had, and it was a surprise to realize she seemed to be very good at making love.

With Seth.

It was funny how it all worked when two people just clicked. She seemed to know where to touch him and he wasn't afraid to ask what she liked. They were each eager to please, desperate to give more pleasure than to take. And in the giving, they received more than expected.

And magic stirred.

But magic dissipated when reality intruded…and reality always intruded. This wasn't, after all, a Disney movie.

Pushing the memory of how he made her feel aside, Leah forced herself to think. The sex was great. She'd expected that but what she hadn't expected was the emotional connection she felt to him while she was in her arms. Something in him, something aside from the heat and the passion and the mind-blowing sex, called to her.

Which was ridiculous because she'd been non-married for a few weeks, who felt emotionally connected to another man shortly after being cheated on? Who did that? Someone who was confused and bemused, hurt and emotionally bruised.

Except that she wasn't, dammit.

She'd never been more clear thinking in her life. Yes, she was angry at Heath, she had every right to be, he'd treated her like trash. But she wasn't hurt or pining over him or crying over or missing him. Even at the height of her betrayal, she'd been more humiliated than hurt, more angry than betrayed. Mostly she just felt relieved she'd dodged that matrimonial disaster zone.

Leah acknowledged somewhere deep inside her she still wanted to be part of a couple, to make a life with someone at her side. Was Heath just a stupid mistake—well, yes, sure he was, of course he was—and was Seth the real deal? Was Seth, that pop-up, make her crazy man, someone she wanted in her life? Was she even allowed to be thinking this way? She was, after all, newly out of a stupid, man-related situation.

Heath is over, her heart told her. *Forgotten about, done.*

It's too soon, her mind insisted, *you're projecting, transferring...acting crazy. It's the dopamine making you stupid.*

Seth's the real deal...

Heart.Head.Heart.Head.Heart.Head.

Leah flopped backward on her bed and flung her arm over her eyes. The crazy train was pulling into her station...

Chapter Eight

AFTER A NIGHT short on sleep and long on soul-searching, Leah rolled over and hit the barrier of a long, hard male body. She was half asleep but she was pretty sure that she went to bed alone. Leah sat up and pushed her hair out of her face. Her eyes focused and, yep, Seth was lying on the bed next to her, his hand supporting his head. Mussed hair, amused eyes, thick arms, washboard stomach and a long, thick…damn, he was wearing boxer shorts.

She'd gone to bed alone and locked the door behind her. Leah looked across the room and, yep, her door was open.

"Practicing your B&E skills?" Leah croaked.

"It's always good to have a backup career. I told you, they come in handy occasionally." Seth drawled, placing his hand on her bare hip.

Leah looked down and realized that she was still wearing his t-shirt and she'd neglected to put panties on. Seth's hand, running over her hip and down her butt told her he appreciated her lack of underwear.

"Hi," he murmured, his eyes a smoky green.

"Hi back," Leah said, sitting up. "Um…what are you doing here?"

Seth placed his hand on her knee. "I finished my business around twelve thirty—the time differences are a bitch—and I thought I'd clear the air but first I had to pick my way through your door. Then I found you conked out."

"Okay," Leah said, "why did you feel the need to clear the air? You didn't do anything wrong."

"Not wrong but maybe I was a little abrupt," Seth replied. "I wasn't expecting you in the shower and by the time we finished, I knew that Stone would be calling me back to discuss a…sensitive issue.

"I owe you an apology." Seth's voice was rough but she heard the sincerity in every word.

That being said, Leah was so conscious of his hand on her thigh, the muscles in his arms, his citrus-spice-Seth smell.

"I could've explained better. You make me crazy," Seth ruefully admitted.

Leah knew how that felt.

"You make me do things, say things, feel things that I'm not accustomed to doing, saying, feeling. That's probably why I've subconsciously avoided you all these years." Seth continued, linking his big hand around the back of her neck. "I don't want to hurt you, Leah. You've been hurt enough. I don't want this to cause you any heartache or pain or any regret."

"I appreciate the sentiment, Seth, but I'm not going to ask you for more than you can give," Leah said as she gripped his arm with one hand.

Seth tensed at her touch and her eyes dropped down and she saw the movement in his shorts. His erection grew thicker, harder, and she swallowed, wishing she were brave enough to make the first move again.

"I want you," he said, his eyes on her mouth, his hand gripping her thigh.

"I know." And for now, it was enough. "I want you, too."

Seth's face turned serious. And determined. "The thing is… sex can lead to complications, emotional complications."

"For me or for you?"

Seth didn't answer her, not that she expected him to. "There are reasons why I think we should keep our distance."

"Yeah, yeah… we live on different continents, my disastrous non-marriage, you might lose focus or become distracted, we might find ourselves wanting more." Leah waved her hand between them. "But we could also be hit by a meteor strike in ten minutes. You might have a heart attack—"

Seth snorted and she had to agree. She'd never met anyone less likely to fall over from a coronary than Seth but she was trying to make a point here.

"I might go to work, meet someone and fall in love at first sight. I might get T-boned by a delivery truck—" Seth looked horrified and his reaction caused her stomach to jump. "My point is that anything could happen and I don't want to regret not taking this time with you. We might have two days or two weeks but I'd like to spend whatever time we have together. Carpe diem, you know?"

Seth placed his hand in the center of her back, silently urging her to scoot closer. She lay down so she faced him and placed her arm across his chest. Seth pulled her into him and tucked her head under his chin. Leah relished the feeling of holding him, touching him, sharing this moment with him. She'd spoken the truth. She didn't know how much time they had but she wanted to be with him. In every way she could.

"Jed's going to kill me." Seth's voice rumbled over her hair and she heard the amusement beneath the words.

"I promise to say nice things at your funeral."

Seth rolled her over so she straddled him and she gasped when her clit settled on his erection, his warmth burning into her despite the barrier of his boxer shorts.

Leah fell forward and their mouths aligned so Leah dropped an open-mouth kiss on his lips before pulling away. "Does this mean what I think it means?"

Seth's eyes glittered. "If it means that I'm going to slide inside you, then yes."

"Did your condoms accompany you on your lock picking adventure?" Leah whispered, nipping his ear lobe and then soothing the small sting with her tongue.

"I'm a boy scout, I always come prepared."

Leah laughed and then went back to the serious business of exploring underside of his jaw with her lips and tongue.

SETH STOOD AT her grandmother's rolltop desk, all his attention on the papers lying on the top. Leah pushed her shoulder into the doorframe of the study, happy to watch him. She was making memories, she thought. When Seth left, and he would leave, she would remember him here, the morning sunlight bouncing off his hair, his long neck, his masculine profile. She'd remember his shoulders were broad and his legs long, and she'd remember the ways the muscles in his arm moved under his tanned skin as he picked up and discarded a piece of paper, when he tapped something into his laptop computer.

She'd remember the way he looked and his masculine scent but most of all she'd remember the way he made her feel. Living with Seth, loving Seth made her feel like a woman, in every sense of the word. She felt powerful but protected, sexy and strong.

Around Seth she felt like the best version of herself. Yes, he could be autocratic and annoying but she sensed behind the walls he'd carefully erected was a man who would be, if he allowed himself to, a fantastic lover. Oh, not in the make-her-scream way—he showed her, often, how good he was at sex—she was talking about being one half of a whole. He would be an amazing partner, strong when he needed to be but happy to allow her to do her own thing.

He was a man, in every sense of the word. Responsible, smart, fully adult. And, unlike Heath, Seth didn't need, or want her money. He didn't require her to cook, to do his laundry, or pay his bills.

All he wanted from her from her company. And, naturally, sex. Lots and lots of sock-blowing-off sex.

Leah didn't have a problem with either concept.

"Are you just going to stand there and stare at me?" Seth

asked softly. "Or are you going to share that mug of coffee?"

Leah didn't bother to ask how he knew she was there or that she was carrying coffee. Seth's kids would have a hell of a time pulling the wool over his eyes. Seth's kids...Was it crazy to wish his kids could be hers, too?

She could see them getting old together. She could see them walking on the beach, a toddler between them, swinging from their hands. She could see them living in this house, raising their kids here, living and loving and arguing.

Her imagination was on steroids. Thinking those thoughts, dreaming those dreams was the romantic equivalent of handing Seth a razor and asking him to slice away at her heart. Seth was not a man a girl should dream about, he wasn't husband or father material. He lived another life a long way away; he had a career that was demanding and exciting and that left no room for a relationship. It certainly had no room for her.

His life and hers could not merge; it was an impossibility. So dreaming dreams and creating scenarios was just silly. A waste of time and energy.

When Leah reached Seth, she placed the mug into his hand. Standing next to him, she laid her palm on his back and tipped her head so her temple rested on his shoulder. Yeah, she should be pulling back, creating some distance between them and she would, later. Right now, she just wanted to be close to him.

Making memories. That was all she was doing.

Seth sipped his coffee and Leah looked down at the crude, one dimensional sketch of an older man, which was lying face up on the desk.

"Who is this?" She picked up the paper and frowned at the image.

Seth plucked the sketch from her fingers and slid it into a paper folder. "That's someone I've been looking for a long time. Unfortunately, the sketch is pretty generic, he could be anyone."

Leah placed her butt on the edge of the desk and stretched out her legs. "Why have you been looking for him?"

"He's a bad guy and I don't say that lightly."

"Talk to me, Seth."

Seth hooked the office chair with his ankle and rolled it towards him. He sat down in the chair and rested his elbow on Leah's thigh. He tapped the folder with his index finger before speaking again. "He really is a son of a bitch. He's the one who is recruiting young people into cults, who made contact with Fayed Khan. He's a master of luring them in; he knows exactly what buttons to push. Whatever the teenager wants the most, he promises that they will get it in A, B, or C cult." Seth saw the shock of her face because he nodded and continued. "Yeah, he has no loyalty to one cult or organization. If the cult wants girls and they can pay, he gets them girls. If a kid wants to join a holy war, he'll find him a place to fight. Provided he can pay for The Recruiter's services."

"But…teenagers?'

"They're young and impressionable and, best of all, they want to buy whatever he is selling, which is, essentially, a place to belong." Seth rubbed his eyes with his fingers. "We've found quite a few of the kids he lured into crappy situations."

"Did you get them out of the situation?" Leah asked.

"Some, we did. Some were eighteen by the time we found them and they didn't want to leave and we couldn't force them to. One or two were in a very bad way."

"Dead?"

"No, but we've had those, too."

Seth's fingers slid up and under Leah's skirt and drew patterns on her skin. There was nothing sexual in his touch; he was just looking for a connection.

Leah reached out and touched his hair, allowed her fingers to skim down his strong neck. "Sorry, Seth."

Seth shrugged. "It's part of the job.'

Leah didn't take his cool tone personally; she knew he was embarrassed he'd allowed her to see his emotions.

Leah picked up the folder and pulled out the sketch and took another look. Putting the folder on the desk, she held the paper and frowned at the image. It wasn't a great representation but the similarities were there. It could be the man she had lunch with, the person who said he was Seth's father.

"Seth this sketch… he could be your father."

"He doesn't look like the photo you sent me, Leah."

"I know but…Show me the photo; it's on your phone, isn't it?"

Seth lifted his phone, found the app, and the picture of his so-called father popped up on his screen. He held the screen up.

Leah put the sketch next to the picture and she shrugged. "It's not anywhere near an exact match but there are similarities."

"Same eyes, same shape of the face…" Leah added.

Seth studied the sketch and picture and nodded once.

"I'm sending the photo to Jett," Seth said, tapping his phone. A minute later he lifted the phone to his ear, his eyes on Leah's face. "Jett? Are you still with Fayed?"

After waiting for Jett's response, Seth spoke again. "I've just sent you a photo of a guy. Ask Fayed if he recognizes him."

Seth held her eyes while he waited for Jett's response and Leah saw the answer on his face before he spoke the words.

Shit. Crap. Damn. Seth's father, the man she'd had lunch with, was the same man who'd lured Fayed away, the same guy Seth was chasing.

"Seth…"

Leah watched the blood in his face drain away. She wanted to hold him, wanted to chase his pain away, but she knew if she touched him, he would shatter in a million pieces.

Just like the ceramic coffee mug he threw at the wall.

★ ★ ★

SETH FELT LIKE his stomach wanted to rocket out of his throat. Could his father, the person who'd contributed half of Seth's DNA, be a raging, crazy, intelligent psychopath who'd lured hundreds of kids into situations that were dangerous and destructive?

At the very least, he had to think it was a strong possibility. In a minute or two, when he was able to think this through, he'd shove the emotion aside and figure out what to do next, work out what Ben's motives were, but right now he needed to work through his anger and his disappointment and, yes, the pain bubbling away in his chest.

"Is this man your father, Seth?"

"There's a good chance that he is."

"When last did you see him?" Leah asked, her voice soft but devoid of pity.

If he'd heard pity he would find another cup to toss. Seth looked at the coffee-covered wall, thought about apologizing but then realized Leah didn't give a crap about her dirty wall, the broken cup, or the stained carpet. Her expression told him she was worried about him. Just him.

He couldn't remember when last a woman had looked at him with compassion in her eyes, looking like she wanted to soothe his wounds, suck out his pain. He'd never allowed any woman to see beyond his tough, oh-so-capable shell and the knowledge Leah was looking at the mess beyond the shell made panic join the nausea in the back of his throat.

"Talk to me, Seth. You need to."

He'd always chosen to act rather than to talk, to take his frustrations out on a punching bag or at the gym. By pushing his body to the limit, he'd tired himself out so he didn't have to think, to talk, to work through his issues. A lifetime running from his father created a shit load of issues…a lack of trust, self-sufficiency, and emotional unavailability. But he liked his issues, he was comfortable with them and he knew his issues shaped his life. He pursued justice, he wanted to rebalance the scales of right and wrong, he wanted to restore the lost or the stolen—art, secrets, people—to the proper owners.

Leah's wide eyes and empathetic expression encouraged him to slice open that mess and bleed on the floor. He didn't know if he could but, for the first time ever, he wanted to. He needed to. The thought was equally liberating and terrifying.

"I only have memories of my father yelling." Seth looked up at the ceiling as he spoke. "And it was always about me, normally because my mom tried to discipline me. In the commune, woman didn't tell men what to do, even if they were only four years old."

Leah stiffened but she didn't speak.

"My mom stumbled into the group when she was eighteen and she married my father three months later. It wasn't long before she realized she'd made a huge mistake. I don't know many of the details of the cult, what they did or who they worshipped, I just know that my father threatened to kill my mother if she left and that she believed them."

"But she did leave." Leah rested her elbows on her thighs and placed her chin in the palm of her hands.

"We left once. He found us and brought us back. We left again and we spent the next fourteen years running. She genuinely believed that if she left and he found her, she would be killed and I would be taken back and brainwashed." Seth rubbed his hand over his face. "We lived in so many towns, I had so many identities, I went to so many schools."

"But he didn't find you."

"He did, eventually. When I joined the army, I used my real name because I was sick of hiding out. If my father wanted me, I thought he could come and take me on."

Seth picked up a pen and tapped it against a folder. "In the army, I got letters from him. He demanded that I come back to them, that I was needed, that they needed me. He promised me wealth and girls and more sex than I could ever dream of, with a different girl every night if that was what I wanted. And that any sexual needs or fantasies I had could be accommodated…"

Leah wrinkled her nose. "Yuck."

"Yeah, apparently nothing was taboo."

"God."

"Trust me, that bunch had nothing to do with God," Seth said, bitterly.

Seth looked up and into her compassionate face, and he felt the fist, encircling his heart, relax its python-like grip.

"So you haven't seen him since you were four?"

Seth looked down, wondering whether to lie. He'd never told anyone that after he left the military he'd tracked his father down—he'd still been living at the compound—and had a come-to-Jesus talk with him. Entering the compound and breaking into his house had been child's play and the conversation he'd had with his father had been short and sweet. Actually, a conversation suggested there had been a dialogue of sorts. Since his hand had been around his father's throat, Seth had done all of the talking.

The message had been simple—Seth wanted nothing to do with him. Ever.

"I met him once. During that…encounter… he realized I wasn't interested in anything he had to offer, or to say."

"And you haven't heard from him since?"

"I heard about his death a few weeks after that."

Leah placed her foot on his thigh and he gripped her ankle, his fingers encircling her slim joint.

"The Recruiter popped up around ten years ago, about six months after I heard about my father's car accident." Seth dropped his hand and he jerked his body up as a thought occurred to him. Oh, fuck.

It made sense, twisted and psychotic, but still sense. "He became The Recruiter because of me."

Leah looked horrified. "What? No, it's not your fault that he's a psychopath!"

When she defended him it felt like his heart was wrapped in a warm blanket. "My rejection of him, of his lifestyle, was the trigger. He started recruiting kids because he couldn't recruit me and every kid he pulled into a cult—it didn't matter which one—was a substitute for me."

Leah rolled her index finger, gesturing for him to keep talking.

"But what was the point if I didn't know what he was doing? The thrill would be sweeter if I knew what was happening and couldn't prevent it. The thrill would even be greater if I started hunting him, that way he could get my attention."

"Your father is seriously screwed up." Leah commented.

"Yeah, but this fits. This makes sense to me." Seth pushed his chair back, stood up, and crossed his arms.

Leah hopped off the desk and busied herself with clearing up the mess on the surface. She picked up the sketch and opened the folder to slide it back into place. Instead of flipping the folder closed, she stared down at the sketch.

"What are you thinking, Leah?"

Leah tapped the nail of her thumb against her teeth before sending him a grim smile. "That he's definitely got your attention now."

Seth stood up and tuned her around, his hands on her bare thighs, pushing up and under her flouncy skirt. "I'm sick of talking about him and my crappy past. Let's do something else."

Leah smiled slowly and he felt his heart bump off his chest. Yeah, she was the best distraction, his favorite way to get out of the swamp in his head. Seth yanked her towards him and slanted his lips over her, his mouth capturing whatever smart aleck comment she'd been about to say. Losing himself in the heat and wonder of her, his tongue slid into her mouth and he lost the ability to think. Blood drained from his head and it was all he could do to stay on his feet as she kissed every bad memory away. His broad hands snaked up to her chest and then his hands were on her breasts, kneading her nipples and listening to her soft moans urging him on.

Leah whimpered in his mouth, hooked her hands around his neck, and boosted herself up, her legs anchored around his waist and the juncture of her thighs riding his erection. Seth held her easily and, still kissing her, walked her out of the study and into her sitting room where there was soft, large couch, which was perfect for what he wanted to do.

Seth sat Leah on the edge of the couch and pushed her skirt up to her hips, his breath hitching at her long, smooth legs. He knelt on the carpet in front of her and he feasted on her mouth, her neck while his shaking fingers undid the buttons to her shirt, pulling it down her arms while he pleasured her breasts. Impatient with the barriers, he pulled her shirt and bra off and then suckled one tip of a rosy breast and then the other. Leah reached out to return the pleasure but Seth easily captured her wrists and held them behind her back while he built her pleasure.

Seth would remember this moment for the rest of his life. In the half-light of the lounge, the rays of the setting sun poured through the high windows and cast golden shadows over her skin, subtly highlighting her curves. Her hair was tousled and her lips were curved in invitation. For a minute, okay, maybe thirty seconds, he just wanted to look at her, absorb her.

Her panties, thank the Lord, were gossamer thin and one quick twist snapped the thin threads that held the tiny triangle in place.

Ignoring her squeal of protest, he flung the g-string over his shoulder and placed his mouth on her hot, wet mound. Loving her taste, Seth slid a finger inside her and felt her contract. Ignoring her demands to hurry up, he walked the fingers of his other hand up her torso to find her breast, rubbing her nipples for maximum pleasure.

He wanted her to let go, to trust him with this most intimate experience. She was so close, so near to flooding, yet he could feel her hesitancy in the fine tremors that ran through her limbs, the way her buttocks tensed in caution and not in anticipation.

Sighing, he kissed his way up her body and looked into her flushed face."What's the matter?"

Leah bit her lip and he smoothed it with his thumb.

"Talk to me. Don't you like me doing that?"

Leah met his eyes. "It's wonderful but do you?"

Did he like it? What a stupid question! Seth let out a soft laugh. "I love it. Why?"

Leah waved a hand. "I thought men didn't...but then, I was with a man who never kissed me there."

Seth's hand snuggled into her folds and she arched her hips as his finger reentered her. "Leah?"

"Mmm?"

Seth briefly sucked on a pert nipple before dragging his mouth across her belly. "We'll continue this conversation later. For now, shut up and let me get back to what I was enjoying."

Leah arched her back and he vaguely heard her whimper but he was lost in her, her taste, small, lost in the intimacy of what he was doing. This wasn't the first time he'd gone down on a woman but it was the first time with Leah and he never wanted it to end. This was more than oral sex, more than a way to get their rocks off, this felt intimate, important. Giving Leah pleasure, allowing her to fall apart in his arms, on his mouth, was all that was important.

Leah shouted, bucked, and gripped his head to her. He slid two fingers up into her and her inner walls clenched around him. He licked her once and then she went utterly still and he licked her again, smiling against her when she lost her shit. He pumped his fingers, she gushed her pleasure before flinging herself back against the couch, her forearm over her eyes and her body shuddering from her orgasm.

Pleasure he'd given her. Seth felt about a hundred feet tall. He straightened, pulled a condom from his back pocket—he'd taken to carrying one around because Leah just had to look at him and he'd get hard—and, not bothering to undress, dropped his shorts and sheathed himself. He placed his arms on either side of her and slid into her heat and silkiness.

Yeah, this was where he wanted to be. His refuge, his pot at the end of the rainbow, his favorite place in the world.

Leah opened her eyes and smiled at him. "I don't know if I can go again."

Seth leaned forward, kissed her and spoke his words against her lips. "Yeah, you can."

She could. And she did.

Chapter Nine

"HEY, SAM. HOW are you doing?"

Even via Skype, Sam's smile was as bright as the setting African sun and ten times more potent. "Hey, Seth."

"Got some time for me?" Seth asked.

He and Stone's sister were friends, good friends, and they worked extremely well together. She also threw a mean right hook and had a black belt in tae kwon do. Men saw the sexy blonde but few knew that she could kick ass in a fight.

"For you? Always." Sam picked a bottle of water and sipped.

"I need some off the cuff profiling."

"I specialize in off the cuff," Sam replied.

"I think that The Recruiter and my old man is the same person and that this is all about me."

Sam lifted her eyebrows and her gaze sharpened. She looked at him for a long time, her head cocked as she made sense of his words. Seth knew how crazy it sounded, hell, the entire situation had "batshit insane" stamped all over it. But it was what it was and they were paid the big bucks to work with crazy.

Sam lifted a red-tipped nail. "Hold on a sec, I think Stone needs to listen to this."

Seth leaned back in his chair as Sam stood up and left the room. Seth turned to look at Leah. They were sitting at the wooden table on the veranda, Leah to his left and Jett to his right.

Leah, a small frown between her eyes, gestured to the screen. "Who is the supermodel?"

Supermodel? Oh, Sam…yeah, with her long legs, slim body, she could've modeled.

"Samantha Stone. She has a doctorate in criminal psychology and she specializes in deviant behavior. She's an independent consultant who works out of the Pytheon offices."

"Oh." Seth watched as Leah played with the beads on her silver bracelet.

If Jett wasn't present he'd lean over, tip up her chin, and kiss her sexy mouth. Then he'd pick her up, strip her naked, and put her on this table and see if it was as solid as it looked. Seth wiped his hand across his face and wondered why his thoughts always went to sex whenever Leah was around. He hadn't been so preoccupied with getting lucky since he was a teenager…hell, he'd never been this preoccupied.

Try and act like the professional you claim to be, Halcott.

Sam appeared in his monitor again. "Big brother is here," Sam said.

Thank God, they could get down to business. Sam settled behind the monitor and after a quick greeting, Stone disappeared from the screen. Seth presumed he was sitting in his usual spot, on the edge of Sam's desk.

Seth briefly explained where they were in the investigation and what the current theory was. Stone's initial shock quickly passed and he moved to stand behind Sam, bending so he could look into the webcam.

"That would explain the taunting emails and his obsession with Pytheon. Yeah, I think it's a strong possibility." Stone nudged Sam. "What do you think?"

Sam nodded. "The first trigger was you visiting him at the compound and he finally had your attention. And he realized that he really liked your attention and he started to crave it. You obviously scared him enough or he felt threatened enough for him not to engage you directly but he needed to. How could he do that? How could he satisfy his desire for attention, negative or not? He faked his death and started recruiting teenagers who looked like you."

"There were girls and other kids who didn't look like me." Seth pointed out.

Sam shrugged. "Work with me. Recruiting those kids satisfied a need for him for a little while but the need for attention grew, the need for your attention grew in him. And when Pytheon started tracking him, when *you* started tracking him, that would've blown his boots off. Your direct attention was on him again."

"So what changed?" Seth asked. "What made him move from that game onto this one? You have to agree that it's a hell of a departure in MO."

"It has to be another trigger, another life changing event." Sam decided after a moment's silence. "Something has changed in his life, and yours, and that's made him deviate from the game."

"My life is as it's always been. I work."

"Far too much and far too hard," Sam agreed and tapped the top of the pencil against her keyboard. "Something has happened to him. He's let you see his face, let that kid see his face. That suggests he's not worried about being caught or that he doesn't care anymore."

Seth placed his elbows on the table and stared at Sam and Stone's worried faces. "That makes him dangerous."

"He always was dangerous." Stone corrected.

"He wants to close the circle," Leah said.

Seth turned to look at her but her attention was on the birds fighting over the seeds in the hanging feeder.

"Seth has also been his holy grail and he's not leaving this life without reconnecting with Seth and, by reconnecting with Seth, I mean to take him with him. He's not leaving Seth behind." Leah continued.

Silence settled over the outdoor space like a frost-covered blanket. Seth couldn't take his eyes off Leah and watched, horrified but fascinated, as a tear rolled down her cheek. She wiped it away with the tips of her fingers and, without looking at him, or anybody, she pushed back her chair and hastened out of the room. When she disappeared from view, he looked back at the monitor and sighed at Sam's worried expression.

"I think she's right," Sam reluctantly admitted. "Her theory makes sense. He's either suicidal, which I doubt, or he believes he's not going to live long." Sam bit the inside of her lip. "Hearing that he has a life threatening disease could have beena trigger. He wants to end this before fate does it for him. Or it could be something else entirely, something that makes sense to him but not to us."

Seth replied, "We need a plan to flush him out, to speed up the process."

From the time he arrived in Cape Town a couple of weeks back, he'd known—sensed—Leah was inextricably linked to the situation, to him being back in the city. From the moment he first heard about his father and his connection to Leah, he'd known—on a subconscious, gut-deep level—she was part of the situation and that he might, if needed to, have to use her in some way to resolve the situation. It wasn't something he'd actively thought about, it was just what his experience gained in shitty places sorting out shitty situations had taught him.

He sucked in a deep breath. "I have a plan. I'm going to use Leah to get to him."

His heart slammed against his ribs as he spoke the words that he couldn't take back. His idea went against every instinct he had of a man sleeping with a woman he cared for, liked, the woman he might be falling for.

But when he pushed that aside and looked at the situation as the COO of Pytheon, as the man who made the tough decisions, it was the only way to stop The Recruiter.

God, he was risking Leah, putting Leah in danger, to capture his father. Fuck.

Do your job, Halcott. Earn the big bucks they are paying you and make the tough call. Seth knew he had to back himself, back his skills, his training. He'd never let anything happen to her.

"You're going to use Leah, Jed's sister, as bait?" Sam asked, her eyes wide.

"Ballsy," Jett murmured.

"He knows his way to me is through her and our way to him is through her."

Sam sent him a sympathetic look. "It's complicated, a huge risk, Seth. And Jed will not be happy."

Like his affair with Leah, Jed didn't need to know. At least until it was all over and Leah was safe.

"I don't like using people in our operations who haven't been trained." Stone stated, his tone hard. "I especially don't like using people who have a personal connection to us."

And Stone thought Seth did? If he could think of something else, anything else, did Stone really think Seth wouldn't take that option? He didn't want to do this, he had no other choice!

"It's a hard decision, Stone, and not one I want to make but don't have any other options. And…" Seth insisted, running his hand over his face. "I won't be doing this alone…I have Jett, and our local Pytheon operative seems competent. I'm sure he has people who can provide backup. Look, I still need to discuss this with Leah, see if she's on board with doing this. If she's not then arguing about this is pointless."

Leah, a part of him begged, *please dig your heels in, and refuse to do this…*

"She'll be safe. We've all done this fifty times before in a lot worse places. We know how to do this," Jett said and

Seth appreciated his support.

"I'll do it."

Seth whipped around at Leah's firm voice and swore under his breath as she walked back into the room and over to where he stood.

Stone looked concerned. "Are you sure, Leah? If not, we'll get you on the first plane out of there."

Leah lifted her chin. "I'm not going to run. I want this over with. I want my life back." She looked down at Seth and lifted one shoulder. "I'll be your bait."

A part of Seth felt like screaming that she should run but they were just delaying the inevitable. His father wouldn't give up. They needed to stand and fight. But, damn, he was super proud of her. "I won't let anything happen to you."

Leah managed a very small smile. "Because if you do, Jed will use you as shark chum."

Seth wanted to tell her he had no intention of losing her, that he couldn't live in a world that didn't have her in it. They didn't have to be a forever and ever couple for him to care, deeply, about her.

"It's a huge risk," Stone said, his face and eyes worried.

Leah nodded and then shrugged again. "It is, but Seth is right. He targeted me for a reason and I'm the link, the way to end this. Seth once said he has to make hard decisions, well, this is one of them. I'm doing this, it's happening."

Although it was his idea, Seth didn't like it.

At—fucking—all.

"I'M GLAD YOU got arrested."

Leah, lying half on and half off Seth's chest, lifted her head to look at him. She'd been on the edge of falling asleep, properly relaxed from an amazing bout of lovemaking, but Seth's comment jerked her awake.

"Getting arrested was a small price to pay for this." She teased as her fingers ran up and down his ribcage.

Seth squirmed and trapped her hand between his ribs and his arm. So, the big, bad operative was ticklish…good to know.

"Do you know why I was in the hotel bar that night?" Seth asked, his index fingers pushing her hair off her forehead.

When he was like this, with her, she saw another side of Seth, someone who wasn't big and badass. This man, lying in bed with her, was softer, almost gentle, more open than he usually was. The sex was phenomenal, it really was, but peeking behind Seth's emotional armor made her feel like she'd won the lottery.

"Tell me," Leah answered.

Seth never spoke about the past, his or hers, so she was intrigued to hear what he was about to say.

"I had to leave the reception because I, instinctively, wanted to knock the asshat's block off."

"Why?"

"Because I was so effing jealous that he got to take you to bed that night and not me," Seth admitted, his voice barely more than a growl.

Leah felt her heart stutter, stumble, before it sat in the

corner and sighed.

Leah lifted her hand to place it on the side of his face. "I felt your eyes on me as I walked down the aisle. I wanted to look at you but I knew that if I did I might—"

"Might what?" Seth demanded, the tips of his fingers digging into the skin above her left butt cheek.

"Do something stupid." Leah lifted her shoulders and her nipples scraped along the warm skin on his chest. "That's why I avoided you when you came out to see Jed and McKenna. You made me doubt myself."

His eyes gleamed and she smiled at the satisfaction she saw on his face. "Yeah? How?"

"Well, I wondered how I could want to strip you naked and do you on the nearest surface when I was supposed to be madly in love with my about-to-be husband. I told myself that you were a very good-looking guy, that feeling attracted to someone else was normal, that it didn't mean anything." Leah wiggled up his body so they were eye to eye. "That could also be because I was having very infrequent, very crappy sex," she told him.

She hadn't meant to say that but, as she was finding out, Seth was rapidly becoming her best friend, the person she could say anything to. How had that happened? How could she, in such a short space in time—three weeks—feel so connected to someone when she'd hadn't had a quarter of the same connection with the man she intended to spend the rest of her life with?

Seth placed his hand over her breast and squeezed, his thumb sliding over her nipple and sending little bolts of pleasure dancing over her skin.

Seth's arm around her back tightened as he pulled her to him in a quick hug. "You dodged a bullet, Leah."

"I really did."

Despite the threat hanging over their heads, she was having an amazing time, in bed and out, with a man who made her feel stunningly alive and indescribably sexy. She hadn't needed Milo's sex toy gift after her train wreck wedding, she'd just needed Seth.

"You're giggling," Seth said, lifting his fingers to her cheek. "Why?"

"Um…well, I was just thinking about the present Milo brought me after Heath cheated on me and I was thinking that you are so much better," Leah answered, her eyes going to the bedside table where she'd tossed the still boxed, unused vibrator.

Seth, as sharp as a scalpel, immediately rolled over her, yanked the drawer open and pulled out the box containing the sex toy. "He brought you a dildo?" he asked, openly amused.

"That's Milo."

Leah reached for the box but Seth's arms were longer and he just held the box out of her reach. He rolled back, sat up, and pulled the lid off the package. "Let's see how it compares."

Leah blushed. "Will you please put it back?" she demanded, feeling panicky and embarrassed.

"C'mon, it'll be fun."

Jeez, she'd barely had a sex life before he came along and

now he wanted her to play with a sex toy? Leah swallowed and looked at the luminous pink object he pulled from the box. How could she go back to that after he left?

And he would leave.

Oh, she knew that it was easier and safer, emotionally, to find sexual fulfillment with a toy than to take a chance on a man who might hurt her. Hell, she was taking a chance on a man and she knew he would hurt her. He was just in her bed for the sex, in a couple of days, weeks, he'd be gone and, once again, she would be left alone.

With her shocking pink dildo.

Leah felt tears in the back of her throat. She would be left holding the heart that she so badly wanted to give away, desperate for a man, for Seth, to take possession of it, to cherish it…her. She didn't want to play games…sex games, fun games, dating games. She didn't want to play at all. Dammit, she wanted a relationship, a shot of a future with one man who loved her. She wanted the bickering and the late night phone calls when they were apart, she wanted the random "pick up milk" or "meet me in bed" texts. She wanted the inside jokes, to exchange long looks across a crowded room, to slip a hand into his, to kiss him hello. Or goodbye. Or goodnight.

Oh, God, she was having a light bulb moment while her lover held her bright pink vibrator.

Vibrator or not, she wanted to be loved by him so badly. Leah touched the tip of her lip with her tongue, blinking away her tears. Seth was busy inspecting the latex fake-penis, playing with its buttons, and he didn't notice how upset she was. She would give up everything, her life in Cape Town, her businesses, her properties—definitely that damn vibrator—if it meant there was the smallest chance that Seth might love her.

This wasn't about being loved by any man, only Seth would do. He was the only person she could, would, consider spending her life with, changing her world for. And all he wanted, she thought as she watched him play with her sex toy, was sex from her.

Could she pick them or what?

Seth placed the head of the vibrating latex cock against her nipple and she jerked back in surprise. Her eyes met his and she shook her head, scooting back on the bed until she could swing her legs over the side. She needed some space, needed some time to think, to find some much needed perspective. She didn't want to play a sex game with sex toys. She didn't want to play the game at all.

She wanted everything…or nothing. She didn't think she could settle for half-ass, not with Seth.

"Leah? Are you okay?" Leah heard the confusion in his voice.

Leah couldn't look at him, not now. She stood up and walked into the en suite bathroom and for the first time ever, she locked the door behind her. Sliding down the closed door, she placed her head between her knees and begged her heart to change its mind.

You don't want to be in love with Seth.

Of course I don't but I think I am.

You can fall out of love.

I'm going to try but I suspect that's not going to be easy to do.

It's going to hurt so damn much.

I know. I wish I could help the way I feel.

SETH PLACED HIS flat hand on the bathroom door and frowned at the silence behind the door. Something was wrong, he'd said or done something to upset Leah but he was in the dark as to where he'd gone off the rails. Then again, they had been discussing her super brief marriage and that was a subject that came with its own set of land mines. Seth clenched his hand into a fist, about to knock on the door but he pulled away, not sure what he'd achieve if he entered the bathroom.

Leah was a puzzle, a conundrum, a mind-boggling mystery. She was a combination of savvy businesswoman and wild child, tough when she needed to be but never brittle. She was empathetic and sensitive yet she had a strong practical streak that reminded him of Jed. She could be fierce and strong yet feminine and flirty and she fascinated him. He suspected he could live with Leah for six decades and there would still be facets of her he'd yet to explore.

She was unlike anyone he'd ever met, fascinating and mysterious, sexy and sweet. He wanted to dive into her, explore the many worlds that made up her crazy mind, but in order to do that he'd have to lose a little control, open himself up to the possibility of a relationship, to commitment, to lo—God, he couldn't even *think* the word.

Love. He tested it on his tongue. He'd have to allow himself to consider love and being in love and surrendering to love.

Truth? He'd rather be in Syria dodging bullets.

Being a part of a couple, falling into a relationship, scared the shit out of him. There were no damn guarantees that the way he felt right now would be the way he felt in ten days, ten months, ten years' time. And, if by some miracle, Leah felt the same it was far more terrifying to think her feelings might change, that the love he'd come to rely on would disappear. What if she woke up one morning and decided he wasn't what she wanted, that she couldn't live with his annoying habits, with the fact he was a selfish workaholic? What if she couldn't live with a man who sometimes had to make some very tough decisions about whether a man lived or died, who saw the stains of his soul and worried she'd be tainted, too?

Would they be able to manage a long distance relationship and, if not, who would have to relocate? Would she be able to leave Cape Town, because leaving New York would mean leaving his job? Even if he could commit—he couldn't but he was playing the devil's advocate here—how could he ask her uproot her life, give up her career, move continents to be with him?

Seth rested his forehead on the bathroom door and felt like a jackhammer was digging up the back of his skull. There were too many variables and far too many what ifs. The chances of them making it were sliver slim and while he was prepared to risk his ass on slim chances, he wouldn't risk his heart. No, it was better if they stopped the madness now and put some distance between them.

Safer, smarter…and possibly the hardest thing he'd ever had to do in his life.

Chapter Ten

SETH WATCHED AS Jett steered his rented car down the driveway and out through Leah's gates. Seth stood on the stone patio in front of Leah's front door and looked towards the street. The skin on the back of his neck tingled and his heart rate inched upwards. He was out there, Seth thought, watching. Seth did a casual sweep of the road, noticed the few cars parked on the street. They were all empty. Too obvious for Ben. He could be in a bedroom, behind a lace curtain or hidden by the lush, summer foliage in one of the many oak trees that lined the street. But he was close, Seth could feel him.

Because he could, because he knew Ben had eyes on him, he lifted a slow but deliberate middle finger and held it up for twenty seconds. If Ben was out there, he'd be left in no doubt that Seth's feelings hadn't changed. With any luck, his "screw you" would spur Ben to act, hopefully sooner than later.

They needed to wrap this situation up.

Seth sent another hard look down the road, around the neighborhood before stepping back into the house and closing the front door behind him. He couldn't control the situation with Ben but he could sort out the mess he and

Leah had become. He hadn't slept with her last night, he hadn't slept at all, his mind too full of Ben and his crazy and when he wasn't mentally running through the information they had about him, then he was thinking about Leah.

So, his plan to have a quick affair with Leah had backfired badly. Leah was now so much more than a bed-based fling. She wasn't just another hot woman he could walk away from, someone he could easily forget about. She'd snuck under his skin and into his heart.

Seth folded his arms and rocked on his heels. How could he trust what he was feeling? The last few weeks had passed at warp speed and he hadn't had any time to take a breath. This, whatever they had, had developed so quickly, possibly because they'd been thrust into a dangerous situation. Could he be suffering from reverse Stockholm Syndrome; had he just fallen for her because she was under his protection? Whatever he was feeling for Leah was so damn unfamiliar, so intense, he wasn't sure if it was real, whether it could last.

Seth was old enough to realize whatever they had had moved beyond the bedroom for Leah, that she was dealing with some of the same emotions he was. And that raised the question…was what she was feeling for him was real? A month ago she'd been prepared to commit herself to another man, to make the biggest promise to another human being that she could. How could her feelings for Heath change so quickly? Was she just transferring what she felt for the asshat onto him? And how would he cope if she they started a relationship and she realized she wasn't actually as into him as he was her.

How would he cope with her leaving?

And if they survived whatever The Recruiter was plotting, and of course they would, and tried to make this work, how would they overcome the obstacles of having separate careers on two different continents?

God, all this soul-searching gave him a headache.

But he knew what he should do, right now, today. He had to make another tough decision; one Leah wouldn't like and probably wouldn't understand. In order to do his job, to focus on what was important, the only thing that was important—keeping her safe—he needed distance between them. Her life was in his hands. He needed to put a barrier between them so he could do his job and, critically, protect her as he reeled her out as bait. He had to be at the top of his game, he had to stay sharp because when he thought about Leah and the things they did together he lost focus, very quickly.

He also needed to step away from her for his emotional safety because if he kept sleeping with her, kept talking to her, he'd find himself flying before he realized he'd taken the leap.

Flying he could cope with, hitting the rocks and shattering into a million pieces was what he was trying to avoid. He'd allowed this situation with Leah to progress too far, he normally bailed long before this, before the woman became this fascinating, before she became important. He had to walk—run!—away. Today, now. Before it was too late.

Seth straightened his shoulders and ignored the cold lump of dread in his stomach, the erratic thump of his rebellious heart. This was the right thing to do, the only thing to do.

So do it already.

He found Leah in her bedroom, standing next to the bed, her arms crossed as if she was trying to hug herself. He knocked on her doorframe and she slowly turned her head, her eyes wide and wet. Oh shit, he hadn't said anything and she was already emotional? God, he hated tears. Seth wanted to turn around and walk away but he planted his feet and forced himself to look at her as he tried to pull the words up his tight throat.

"Please tell me that this is nearly over," Leah said, her voice saturated with suppressed emotion. "I need to go back to my life."

Seth pushed his shoulder into the frame of the door, looking for support. "I do think it'll be over soon."

Leah sniffed, tossed her head, and looked him in the eye. "And you and I? Why do I think you want to tell me that it's over, too?"

Seth swallowed, massaged his Adam's apple, and forced his tongue to form the words. "Because it is. This…you and I, it's not fun and games anymore."

"No, it's not."

"Leah, I can't. I am not what—"

Leah held up her hand to stop him and, knowing he had the potential to say the wrong thing, he immediately shut his mouth.

"I know what you're about to say. I am not what you need. Like that's a surprise," Leah said, her voice bitter. "I'm never quite what a guy needs."

Oh, crap. She'd grabbed the wrong end of the stick. Seth opened his mouth to refute her words but then he saw the tears rolling down her face and his heart bounced off his chest. He didn't know how to deal with tears and he wanted to kick his own ass.

"Shit, don't cry." He reached forward but wasn't sure what to do with his hands.

"Say it."

Seth briefly closed his eyes. "I do think that taking a break, a breath, would be a good idea."

Leah bit her bottom lip. "You're calling it? Us?"

Seth nodded. "I'm calling it."

Slowly, but inexorably, fury replaced the pain in her eyes. He understood that, anger was easier to deal with than hurt and disappointment.

"Screw you, Halcott! Screw all you stupid men with your commitment issues, your infidelity issues, and your stupid pea-like brains and asinine attitudes."

She was lumping in with her waste of skin ex. Oh, hell no. He was nothing like Heath the asshat. "Don't compare me to him!"

"Why the hell not?" Leah demanded, rubbing the back of her hand against her wet cheek. "He didn't want me, he just wanted my money! You don't want me, you just want sex. As soon as the situation became a bit too real between us, too grown-up, you bail! You are both jerks and I deserve better than either of you."

He couldn't disagree with her. She did deserve so much

better than an ex-soldier with a lot of blood on his hands. "You're right, you do. I'm not what you need, Leah. I'm hard, I've taken lives, I can be a cold, selfish bastard."

"You can also be loving and giving and warm and funny," Leah replied. "I know that you've crossed lines you maybe shouldn't have, Seth, I know Jed probably did the same, as did my father. I love them anyway. I know you've all made decisions that might be morally questionable but I know that none of you made them lightly. You considered every option before you pushed that button, pulled that trigger, issued that order. I know the heart of my father and brother, as I know the heart of you. I'm not an idiot and I'm not naive but I believe in them and I believe in you. I love them and I—"

He couldn't walk away, not if she said it. And he had to walk away.

"Stop!" He barked the word out and Leah, thank God, fell silent.

Seth felt like she swept his feet from under him, like he was falling down Alice's hole, like he was lost and alone in a jungle, surrounded by insurgents. Her unfinished sentence injected paralyzing terror into his system. If she said it, if he heard that particular phrase, he'd crumble right where he stood and risk everything to be with her. He couldn't, wouldn't. So he told her his first lie, the one thing he knew would stop this conversation dead. "I don't love you."

The words hit her like a bullet to her chest and he saw shock chase hurt across her face. "I won't let myself love you, Leah. I can't," he said, his voice low but determined.

He couldn't lose control, not now. Too much was at stake.

"Coward." Leah threw the word in his face and he flinched.

But he held her gaze, held his ground. "I'm sorry you think that, but this has happened too fast and under difficult circumstances. It's easy to be confused about what you are feeling."

"Are you seriously suggesting that I don't know my own mind?"

"I'm suggesting that we've been operating at warp speed in a tense situation, which leads to heightened emotions. Would this have happened in normal life?"

"I can't answer that. It did happen, these were our circumstances. And you're looking for excuses for why this won't work. I want to make it very clear that I am not even a little confused about what I feel for you!" Leah said.

Her tears disappeared as she sucked in determination and pride along with air. There was her father, the hard-ass general. There was the streak of pride that was an essential part of Jed. Oh, yeah, beneath the charm and the empathy and the warmth, his girl had the stiff pride of the Hamilton's. He was proud she was standing up to him but sick at the thought it was the final nail in the coffin he'd constructed.

"I'm not going to beg you to love me, Seth." Leah stated, her voice soft but as hard as tungsten. "If you don't, that's fine. There's no law that says you have to."

Seth, feeling shattered, ran his hand through his hair.

But damn, he had to admire her strength, her pride, her ability to face a situation and deal with it. “You're a hell of a woman, Leah.”

“Yeah, I'm slowly starting to think that I am. Maybe one day I'll meet a guy who can actually commit to me but I'm not holding my breath.” Leah lifted a hand to stop him from speaking. “Would you mind leaving, please? I'd really like to be alone.”

Seth, knowing that there was nothing more to say, left.

★ ★ ★

“I FEEL LIKE I have a broken rib.” Leah told Milo the next day. “I look fine on the outside but every breath I take hurts like hell.”

Leah needed this time with Milo, needed his acerbic comments, his sarcastic approach to life and love. Milo had looked a little shell-shocked and had openly voiced his disbelief he was playing Agony Aunt again and so soon!

But when Seth drop-kicked her heart a few hours earlier, Milo was the person she called. Good friend that he was, he'd dropped everything and belted over.

As soon as he arrived, Seth left and Leah was grateful. She could bitch about him without worrying she'd be overheard. Living in the same house as the man who she loved but couldn't have was a special, special type of horrible.

Milo topped up her wine glass and nodded. “Yep, now this is a broken heart. Heath was just a trial run. Where is the heartbreaker?"

Leah cradled her wine glass to her chest. "He went out and, since we're not talking, he didn't tell me where. I'm surprised he left me alone."

Milo looked offended. "Hey! And what am I? Chopped liver? Seth would never have left you unless I was here."

"Sorry."

"Drink that wine, don't hug it." Milo ordered. "You won't be able to drown your sorrows unless you drink."

"I'm feeling miserable enough already, I don't need to be hungover as well," Leah retorted but she took a sip of wine. "And you need to work on being more sympathetic. Where are the cheesy movies, the ice cream, the endless supplies of tissues?"

Milo rolled his eyes. "You're not crying, you hate cheesy movies, and ice cream makes you fat."

"Why did I have to have a guy and a health nut for a best friend?" Leah asked the ceiling.

Milo sent her a tough look and leaned forward, his face serious. "I'm not going to pat your hand and tell you that the sun will come out tomorrow or that there are plenty of fish in the sea. Honestly, and unfortunately, I think Seth is your big catch, and he will always be the one who got away."

"I wonder when the comforting is going to start?"

Milo ignored her sarcasm. "You're feeling sad and that's okay—"

Leah disagreed. It was anything but okay.

"Your pain is a human experience but it will pass. One day, hopefully sooner or later, you'll wake up and it won't hurt so much. The day after that it'll hurt a little less."

"That can't happen soon enough," Leah muttered into her wine. She glared at Milo and swatted his comforting hand off her knee. "When are you going to start trashing him?"

She and Milo had spent many hours trashing Heath and she thought Seth deserved the same treatment.

Milo, however, didn't. "I don't think I can. Heath was a prick but Seth, not so much. He was honest with you, Lee. He didn't lead you on and when he thought he was getting in too deep, he bailed. He didn't lie to you, cheat on you, mess you around. I really like the guy."

So did she, dammit. And Milo was right. All Seth had done was to choose to not have a relationship with her. She might not like it but he was allowed to do that. It was his prerogative to choose whether to be committed to someone or not. God, she hated that she could be so very sensible, reasonable. It didn't help her bruised and battered heart; it was still hiding out in the darkest corner of her ribcage, struggling to survive.

She met Milo's sympathetic eyes and sighed. "I like him, too."

"Well, the only thing you can do right now is to drink. Have some more wine."

Leah watched as Milo poured red wine into her fat glass. "I wish he'd love me, Mi."

"I think he does, hon. In his way or as much as he can, or allow himself to."

Leah blinked away tears and sent a longing look to the

kitchen. "Can I have ice cream now?"

"No, drink your wine." Milo told her and turned around when he heard the front door open.

Milo immediately stood up and grabbed the heavy base of the lamp on the side table closest to him and held it like a baseball bat. Leah gasped, not only was the lamp one of her favorites, it was also a rare French 1930, art deco lamp signed by Max Le Verrier.

"Put that down." She hissed.

"Seth said to look after you and that's what I'm doing." Milo snapped, his eyes on the door and his white fist clutching the lamp.

"I doubt a criminal would enter through the front door using a key," Leah said and tried to take the lamp from his hand to put it back on the table. The cord was stretched tight and she really didn't want to have to do any re-wiring. She could, she just didn't want to.

Seth appeared in the doorway to the sitting room. He looked from Milo and Leah and back to Milo again.

"What'cha doing?" he drawled.

Leah tugged the lamp away and replaced it on the table and cursed when she saw the wiring had pulled away from its connection. "Milo thought you were an intruder and he was going to brain you with the lamp."

Seth tossed his wallet and keys onto the coffee table and looked at the lamp. "Not a bad idea. Solid base, good weight but awkward."

"It's an expensive lamp and over eighty years old." Leah hotly protested.

"I think we can all agree that you are worth more than the lamp." Seth quietly stated before nodding towards the fireplace. "The poker would be a better weapon though. Longer reach, lighter, easier to handle."

Milo pushed a hand into his blond hair. "I'll remember that." He glared at Leah. "Then again, I might just save the lamp."

Leah winced at his tart tone and heard a tinge of hurt. Realizing that she'd been a bit of a bitch, she put her hand on his bicep and squeezed. "Sorry. I know that you were looking after me but I knew it was Seth."

"How?"

Leah looked at Seth who was standing on the other side of the coffee table, his feet spread wide and his big arms crossed.

"How what?" she asked, confused.

"How could you be sure it was me?"

"Because bad guys don't use the front door!" Leah retorted. "That's Sneaky Behavior 101!"

Seth exchanged a long, frustrated look with Milo before closing his eyes. "God," he muttered.

Milo shook his head at Leah and lifted her hands in a "what have I done?" gesture. She'd sensed Seth's arrival long before he even put the key in the door. Neither of them would understand that, no matter how old she got or how far apart they lived, she was forever tuned into to his frequency, into his vibe. Leah opened her mouth to explain and, when she saw their irritation, she snapped it shut again. What was the point?

Seth had made it very clear they'd had their time. That whatever they'd had, was over. He wouldn't be interested in her metaphysical, slightly kooky, explanation.

"Since my body-guarding skills are no longer needed here, I'm going to go," Milo said. He dropped a quick kiss on Leah's cheek and she took the opportunity to whisper a quick "sorry" in his ear. Milo just replied with a sardonic "mmm."

Seth saw Milo out and Leah heard the snap of the lock on the front door. She picked up her wine and looked at Seth when he walked back into the room. He rested his arm on the mantel above the fireplace and looked down into large copper bowl filled with dried out pine cones that filled the space in summer time.

Was what they had really over? How could it be when desire and longing filled every look they exchanged? How was she supposed to let that go, let him go? But how could she get him to stay? Oh, she knew he had to go back to New York but that didn't necessarily mean he needed to leave her life. Milo could manage her business, she trusted him to look after her properties. And it wasn't like she couldn't fly back whenever she needed to...this didn't have to end. She could leave with him or she could stay, they could have a long distance relationship...talking every night, visiting each other when they could. It wasn't impossible. There were so many ways they could be together, so many plans that could be made.

How could she persuade him to consider any or all of them?

"Don't do this, Leah."

Leah heard the command in his voice and glared at his back.

"Do what?" she asked, trying to keep her voice light.

"You're trying to find a way around this situation, around us. I'm not going there," Seth replied.

He dragged a hand across his face and Leah noticed he looked exhausted. She knew she was.

"I wish you didn't have to be bait for Ben. I'm hoping that he'll just contact me directly and leave you out of it."

That was a nice dream but they knew there was no chance of that happening.

"He won't." Leah told him.

"Why do you say that?" Seth asked, looking at a photo of her and her mom that was taken shortly before her death.

Leah gripped the back of her chair and dug her fingernails into the fabric. In the muted light he looked like a strong and powerful and pissed off warrior. And hot. So very hot, so very sexy.

Leah pushed her hair back from her face and forced her thoughts off getting Seth naked. "He wants your attention, I agree with that, but he also wants to make you suffer. Contacting you and asking you to meet is too damn easy. It won't fulfill his objective of getting you back under his command."

Seth's expression turned grim. "And the only way he'll get that if he has you. He knows I'd do anything for you."

Anything? *Anything?* Hardly! "That's not true but, yes, he doesn't know that."

Seth frowned. "I would do anything for you, Leah."

Leah shook her head and sucked her bottom lip between her teeth. "Anything means anything, Seth, and we both know that's not the truth. You won't love me, you won't trust me, you won't let me love you."

Seth jerked his head back as if she'd slapped his face. "I don't know how to love you! I don't know how to love anybody! I don't know how to be loved," Seth said, his voice quiet but determined.

God, that he thought that made her feel so damn sad.

"That's rubbish, Seth. There isn't a formula to loving me, a manual you have to follow. You wake up, kiss me good morning, or make love to me, if that's what we want to do. One or the other makes coffee, we have breakfast, we go our separate ways. We meet up again, chat, talk, eat dinner, go to bed and make love. I bring you aspirin if you have a headache, you buy me flowers if you feel the urge. We eat out and we argue about movies we want to watch—I love sci-fi by the way—you cook, I clean. I cook, you clean. We cook together, we clean together."

"Leah—"

Oh, no, she needed to finish this. "On weekends, we head to the country or the beach. We fly to Rome or LA if we feel the urge. We don't lie, we don't cheat, and we communicate often. I don't know how it will work out, just that it will, that it can!"

Seth gripped the bridge of his nose and stared at the floor. "You make it sound so damn easy."

And he made it sound so impossible. "It is easy." Leah

insisted. "You just have to decide that it's what you want."

"We live on different sides of the world, Leah!"

That was the best argument he had? What a rookie. "I'd move. Milo would run my business for me and I could fly back when I needed to."

If she wasn't feeling so shattered, Leah would've laughed at his stunned face.

"You'd do that for me?"

Leah dredged up a smile and forced it onto her face. "Yeah, I would. But then again, I would do *anything* for you, Seth."

He turned his head to look at her and Leah saw the confusion in his eyes, the naked want warring with his control.

She decided to risk the question. "Would it be the worst thing in the world? You and I?"

"No. The worst thing in the world would be having you in my life and then losing you."

His harsh words hovered in the air between them and Leah held his anguished eyes. "I'm scared, too, Seth."

Seth's mouth opened as if he were about to speak, to cave, and Leah held her breath, hoping he'd say or do something to give her some hope, a slight hint that she might have a chance. Behind the frustration and the control and the pride, she thought she saw his vulnerability, his desire to make this work. Then the naked need in his eyes faded and Leah knew she'd lost him. She'd lost him to his fear and to his need to be in control.

He wasn't in the right state of mind to love her and she doubted he ever would be. Seth wasn't willing to fall in love because—hell, it wasn't about her and whether he could love her—he just wasn't prepared to allow himself to fall in love. He wasn't prepared to be vulnerable, to let her into those secret places in his mind and heart.

She needed to walk away, she had to walk away. She needed to let go of him, stop this craziness from scouring her heart and soul. Loving Seth made her feel uncertain, unworthy, lost. Like she did after her marriage fell apart.

Enough now.

She'd miss Seth. She'd miss everything about him. But no matter how much she loved him, she had to love herself more. She needed to get over him and to do that she had to walk away, put herself first.

It had to end. Right now, this minute.

Leah took a deep breath. "I need this situation resolved, Seth. I need you out of my house and out of my life." Leah looked at him and lifted her hands. "You won't fight for me and I'm so over fighting by myself, constantly looking for a way to make you stay."

"I'm not doing that anymore, Seth. And I damn sure will, one day, be over you." Leah touched her top lip with her tongue and met his narrowed eyes.

Leah picked up the dirty glasses and the bottle of wine. "I'm going to bed." She stopped at the door and turned back to look at him. "Sort this out, Seth. I need this to be over."

Chapter Eleven

JETT REMOVED A tiny earpiece from its bed of foam and Seth watched as he walked to Leah and pushed her hair behind her ear.

"If something happens to you, we can track you and you can listen to us," Jett said as he inserted the flesh-colored earpiece into her ear.

Seth nodded, satisfied that it was nearly undetectable.

"So I can hear you but you can't hear me?'

Jett shook his head then nodded to her watch. "Seth placed a blue tooth mic into your watch. Whatever you say, we'll hear."

Leah managed a small smile. "So I get to lift my wrist like the secret service guys do in the movies?'

Jett laughed. "This is high tech, you just have to talk normally and we'll hear you."

Seth couldn't laugh or smile. He was having a hard enough time keeping his stomach from flying up his throat every time he thought about Leah leaving the house without him, tempting his waste-of-DNA father to snatch her. Because they all knew that was exactly what Ben would do at the earliest opportunity. Ben hadn't contacted him directly, that was way too easy, and they all knew he was waiting for an opportunity to inflict as much damage as possible. He knew Leah was his weak link and, as Leah had suggested, Ben wanted to make him suffer. And it was working.

Seth raked a hand through his already messy hair. This is why an operative shouldn't become personally involved in volatile situations. And hell, no matter how much he tried to deny it, he was involved. He was neck-deep involved with Leah and he felt like he was walking into an ambush blindfolded and unarmed, waiting for the bullet to rip him apart.

Seth turned away and looked out of the window of the lounge, staring at the ocean. God, why did love have to come with such uncertainty? He was terrified if Ben took her, they wouldn't get to her quickly enough, and that he would hurt her in order to hurt Seth. Seth ground his teeth together. If Ben put a finger mark on Leah, Seth would rip his limbs off, one by one. He was scared for Leah, but loving Leah scared him as much. The uncertainty of love terrified him. Like this operation, so much could go wrong. Like baiting Ben, love was dangerous. It meant exposing himself, taking a chance, trusting that it would work out.

"So, I have to do this every time I go out?" Leah asked, distracting him from his whirling thoughts.

"Yep, now that our backup agents are here, we can you use as bait," Jett said. "Hopefully, it won't be too long before he makes a move."

"God, I hope he does, and quickly. I need this to be over with." Leah said. Leah turned to look at Seth. "How long do you think this will take?"

"How long is a piece of string?" Seth replied. "I really

don't know but I don't think he'll hang around. If we give him a decent opportunity, he'll act."

It wasn't something he could quantify. This situation, his gut was telling him, would be over in a week, two at the very most.

Leah touched her ear that contained the earpiece and Seth shook his head. "Don't touch your ear, it's an instant giveaway that you are wired."

Jett folded his arms across his chest. "If he has a brain in his head then he'll assume that. He knows you won't leave her without protection, without knowing where she is at any given moment. This is just part of the game. He wants to connect with you, but he wants Leah, so he has some form of control over you."

"Because he knows there would be a good chance of me blowing his head off if I had him alone," Seth said.

Instead of looking horrified at his matter-of-fact statement, Leah tipped her head and looked contemplative. "Is that a possibility?"

Seth sent her a steady look, knowing what she was asking whether shooting his father would be one of his "hard" decisions.

He shook his head. "I'd like him to spend the rest of his miserable life in solitary but I'll be satisfied if he's off the streets. But if there's a choice between his life or yours, or mine, or one of my men's, then all bets are off and I will take him out." Seth saw the worry in her eyes and realized Leah was more concerned about him, his state of mind rather than the precarious situation she'd volunteered herself for. "I don't think of him as my father. I never had a father and he's not mine. I have no emotional connection to him."

Leah bit her lip and eventually nodded. "Then you won't suffer any guilt or misplaced emotion about arresting him or, God forbid, hurting him?"

"No."

He absolutely wouldn't. All he cared about was ending this nightmare, getting Leah home safe and sound. If anything happened to her then he would live with that eating him up from the inside out for the rest of his life and beyond. He could lose Ben, he'd never had him, but he absolutely refused to lose Leah. She was…

Aw, shit, why was he fighting this? Why not just admit it? She was his everything. She was the place his soul ran to looking for peace, the beat of his heart. He didn't want to live without her, be without her in any shape or form. He was sick of his life lived in stasis, of just existing, functioning. He wanted the ups and downs, the crazy and the soft. The normal and the bizarre bits of love and life. He wanted it with her.

Seth opened his mouth to tell her, to say something but Jett spoke first. "Right, Leah, you need to leave. Your yoga studio is a couple of blocks over, are you going to walk or drive?"

Leah picked up her gym bag and her yoga mat. "What do you suggest?'

"If you walk he has a better chance of taking you. If you drive, not so much…it'll delay the process."

Seth noticed her trembling fingers and her wobbling lip.

He felt a spurt of pride when she straightened her shoulders and sent Jett a weak grin.

"Let's give him the best chance possible. Let's get it over with."

"That's my girl,' Seth said, walking up to her and placing a hand on her shoulder.

Leah stepped back and her eyes turned frosty. "But I'm not, am I? Your girl?"

Seth rubbed his hand across his mouth. He darted a glance at Jett, wondering whether he should tell her that he was over his quest to be alone, that he wanted more. That he wanted everything. Then he remembered where they were and what they were doing and he hardened his heart.

"We need to park the emotions, Leah." Seth ordered, his tone rock hard. "This isn't the time to get into that. We need to get our shit together and concentrate on the mission."

He saw the hurt in Leah's eyes and he wanted to explain his years of training made him able to shove away his emotions and focus. It was better not to say anything. He walked over to the table and picked up the spare ear piece and shoved it into his ear. He pushed a button on his watch and looked at Leah, who was clutching her yoga mat as if her life depended on it.

"Earpiece working?"

Leah slapped her hand against her ear and that was confirmation that the device was working. "Don't flinch, don't jump, pretend to ignore it. I'll keep communication to the minimum but just remember I have your back. Nothing is going to happen to you."

Leah lifted her chin. "It had better not or Jed and my father will skin ten layers of skin off you."

Seth winced, knowing that to be the truth. "Yeah, maybe we should neglect to tell them about this." He nodded to the hall. "Go on now, we'll be behind you. Trust us, Leah, trust me."

Leah nodded and emotion filled her eyes. "I do. I just wish you could do the same for me."

★ ★ ★

ALL IN ALL, it was a bit anticlimactic, Leah thought, standing next to Ben in the rotating cable car as it slowly climbed Table Mountain. It took four days of her walking to yoga, to the shops, before a small white car pulled up alongside her. Ben rested the barrel of a pistol on the side of the open widow and, politely, it had to be said, told her get into the car. She complied and within the hour she was standing next to him in the Table Mountain cable car, knowing he kept a firm grip on the pistol hidden in the pocket of his sleeveless, multi-pocketed, khaki jacket.

The car was full of tourists and Leah relaxed a fraction; she doubted he'd shoot her in front of so many witnesses. Come to think about it, Table Mountain was a stupid place to meet. The world-famous tourist attraction was not only busy but it was an area that didn't have many escape routes. The cable car or winding paths were the only ways to get off the mountain.

Leah crossed her foot over her ankles and looked at Ben.

Soon they'd reach the top and the heart-stopping close-ups of the mountain's sheer cliffs, but she took a moment to take in the amazing view of the city bowl, the beaches, and the Atlantic Ocean. "I wanted to bring Seth up here but you've kept us rather busy."

Ben didn't reply. In fact, he'd said little besides telling her what to do and where to go and that he'd shoot her if she shouted for help. His face was hard, cold, and determined and she didn't doubt his word. He looked like he had nothing to lose.

"Angel, we're in the car behind you and we've had eyes on you the whole way."

Leah resisted the urge to place her hand on her ear as relief rolled over her. Every time she heard Seth's calm, controlled voice she felt a little stronger, more convinced they'd all come out of this situation unscathed.

"You're doing great, sweetheart." Seth added.

Angel, sweetheart. Leah briefly closed her eyes. God, what she wouldn't do to hear him call her that for the rest of her life. But that wasn't meant to be, Seth wasn't prepared to take that risk, to jump that high and that far.

"Idiot," she muttered.

Ben lifted his eyebrows at her. "Me?"

"Not you, your son."

"He's not my son, I don't know him."

Leah frowned. "What did you say?"

"I'm not his father. I'm not Ben Halcott."

Leah gasped and gestured to the gun in his pocket. "But then…who are you and why this?"

Ben, or not-Ben, tipped his head back to rest it against the reinforced window. "I owed a man a favor. He's not the type of man you say no to."

"Keep him talking, Leah." Seth stated, his voice calm. "Let's see where this is going."

"So to be clear, you're not Seth's father."

"Apparently Seth's father died in a car accident. The fact that I resemble him, looks-wise, is why I'm in this shitty country at the end of the world."

"It's not shitty—" Leah started to defend her adopted country but realized there were more important things to worry about right now.

Like the fact the car was approaching the station and about to dock. The doors opened and Ben gestured her to step out and, because she had no other choice, she did.

"Where are we going?" Leah asked, following Seth's instruction to find out.

"To the viewing platform fifty meters east of this station."

"Good girl." Seth murmured.

Ben placed an arm around her waist and Leah tried to put some distance between them but he hauled her back to his side. Leah looked around, sighing when she noticed the flat topped mountain teeming with people. Sunset, the most romantic time of day, and a fantastic photo opportunity. And she was in the company of a madman.

This wasn't the best way to visit one of the country's favorite attractions. Bitch Karma obviously had it in for her.

"Doors opening. On our way. Hang tough."

"Tell me you love me. Just once," Leah begged Seth. "Just in case."

"You know damn well that I do. Now fucking concentrate!"

Leah stumbled and Ben's arm kept her from falling flat on her face. Joy and fear swept across her, as wet and as cool as the mist that frequently covered this mountain. What if that was the only "I love you" she ever heard from him? What if fake-Ben had something diabolical up his sleeve, something none of them anticipated? He didn't seem the type to go out quietly and Leah, for the first time since she opened that car door and put herself at his mercy, felt truly scared.

She and Seth had a chance at a happily ever after but it all depended on this sick psycho marching her towards a viewing platform that was virtually empty of people. The best views were further along and that was why people came up here at sunset. Leah pulled in rapid, choppy breaths. She wanted to howl and cry, sink to her knees and beg.

"I need you to be brave for me a little longer, Leah. I can see you and we're approaching. No, don't look around, just walk with him."

Walk with him? Did Seth know what he was asking? Every muscle in her body tensed as they walked the pathway to the platform and then they stepped onto the wooden planks. A young Japanese couple turned as they approached and their easy smiles turned to fear as Ben pulled the gun from his pocket. With a subdued scream they bolted past Leah, feet flying.

"You do know they are going to alert security?" Leah asked him, cursing the fact that her voice sounded shaky.

Ben shrugged and leaned his butt against the wooden and steel railing. He looked unconcerned but his arm around her waist tightened. He also pushed the barrel of the gun deeper into her side.

"This situation will be over long before they arrive. Besides I suspect that Halcott and his sidekick have informed the authorities of the situation." Ben looked past Leah and nodded.

"He's approaching."

He hadn't directed the words at her and Leah realized that, like she was, Ben was communicating with someone. That someone was probably the person in charge of this perverted party. And the fact that Fake-Ben's boss wasn't making a physical appearance scared the crap out of her.

"Who are you talking to?" she demanded.

Ben ignored her and she felt him tense. She lifted her head and saw Seth walking towards them, his pistol up and pointed at where she imagined the center of Ben's forehead to be. Leah flicked a glance to Jett and he wasn't looking at her either, his focus was on Ben, his gun pointed in the same direction as Seth's. Leah tried to move to Seth but the barrel of Ben's gun jabbed her in the kidneys.

Oh, right, she was his hostage. Shit.

"You shoot her and I'll drop you where you stand." Seth growled.

"He's wired," Leah told them. "He's talking to someone else."

Seth looked at her and his glance left her in no doubt that he expected her to shut the hell up.

Seth raised his eyebrow at fake-Ben. "Want to explain what this is about?"

Seth and Jett kept their eyes on Ben, their concentration absolute. But she knew behind their stoic, emotionless faces, they were running scenarios trying to figure out a way out of this mess. There wasn't one, or not a quick one. They could be here for hours and, frankly, she was over having a gun bruising her skin. But she couldn't think of anything she could do or say that would circumvent someone from ending up with a hole or two.

Behind her, Ben's breathing became raspy and his hot breath blew over her hair. "Your father died in that car accident ten years ago. I am not your father."

"Then I don't have the faintest fucking idea why we are on this mountain pointing guns at each other," Seth replied, without a trace of emotion in his voice.

"You are chasing someone, you call him The Recruiter, and he's tired of looking over his shoulder."

Seth's eyes narrowed and he waited for Ben to continue.

"Because of your history with cults, you are the driving force behind his capture. You've come a bit too close to him once or twice and he wants the freedom to continue operating without constantly looking over his shoulder."

"So, meeting Leah and you acting like my father was all a ruse to get me out of the country and away from my support base."

"You were supposed to come up here alone. I was going

to kill her and The Recruiter was going to kill you." Fake Ben stated. "He wasn't expecting you to have backup."

"Not sorry we foiled your plan." Seth sarcastically replied.

"He might still try." Ben's voice took on a desperate quality.

Leah let out a small cry but that damn gun kept her in place. God, Seth was going to die…

Jett's eyes briefly met hers and she saw the reassurance there. "No way," he said. "There are too many people on this mountain for him to shoot Seth. He's bullshitting you."

"Oh." Ben said. Leah felt the gun wobble and the arm around her waist loosen. "He still wants Leah dead." "I'm telling you, The Recruiter isn't going to shoot her or anybody, not in such a public place. That's a risk he'd never take," Seth said, still calm, still steady. *God, he was magnificent!*

"No, he won't because I will shoot her." Fake Ben replied.

God! *Oh God, Oh God, Oh God*!

Seth didn't flinch. "Why does he want Leah dead?" Leah glared at Seth. *Okay, he said those words just a bit too casually!*

Ben listened for a moment and then passed on the message. "You've caused him some trouble, disrupted some operations. He tried to take you out weeks ago. It was supposed to be a random mugging, another violent incident in a country prone to violent incidents."

"Tidy." Seth's eyes didn't move from Ben. "And the mannequin in the pool?"

Ben shrugged. "A creative warning, a way to mess with your head."

"I don't scare easily." Seth said, bored.

Leah felt Ben cock his head, listening to the voice in his ear. "But her dying does scare you. He quite likes the idea of punishing you like that. Depending on his mood, he'll let you have a couple of weeks to suffer before he takes out a hit on you, too."

"Not if I get to him first." Seth retorted.

Ben's mouth lifted in a barely there, sardonic smile. "He says that he was five feet from you earlier and you didn't know him. He's just another tourist on this mountain, you won't find him." Ben pulled in a breath. "He's told me to end this."

"Nobody is going to die today." Seth said.

"She is."

"She is *not.*"

Oh, God, Seth sounded so certain, so in control but tears still rolled down her face. She wanted to believe him but she couldn't. Not while she had a gun bruising her kidneys.

"And so am I. Going to die, that is." Ben shrugged. "By your hand or mine, that's the deal. My life for my daughter's. Leah's life for my daughter's return."

Seth frowned. "Let me get this straight. The Recruiter is holding your daughter and he's been forcing you to jump through these hoops to get her back?" Seth shook his head. "He lied to you. He has no intention of returning her. Nothing you do or say is going to change that."

"It was a chance I had to take, I had to try. I would do

anything for her, even this."

Despite her fear, Leah heard the agony in his voice and felt his despair. "What's her name?" she quietly asked.

"Hope." Ben's voice cracked. "Her name is Hope Frame. She was taken from a club called The Gambler in Chicago. He planned this, every step. He looked for someone who looked like your father, like you, and he stumbled across me. My daughter was his leverage."

"I'll look for her." Seth told him. "If you put down your gun and let Leah go, I'll look for her."

"I *can't.*"

"You can and you will."

Without warning, Ben shoved Leah away from him and she fell to her knees, her hands slamming into the wooden walkway. Leah looked over her shoulder and saw that Ben walking backward, parallel to the railing, the gun still pointed at her back.

Seth spoke again, his deep voice rolling over them. "We can talk this out. I can help you, help Hope. Let me do that."

"No! No! He's going to kill Hope! He's going to kill her in the worst way he can think of!"

Neither Seth nor Jett wavered. They just stood there, weapons raised, cool and in control. "Is he still talking to you?" Seth, lowering his voice.

"Yeah."

Seth lowered his weapon and Leah, her heart in her throat, watched as Seth slowly and oh–so-confidently walked towards Ben. She held her breath, waiting for her world to end but nothing happened. When Seth reached Ben, he twisted Ben's pistol out of his hand and tucked it into the back of his pants. Then he grabbed his sleeveless vest and flipped it open.

Seth took a small microphone off the inside of Ben's vest and lifted it to his mouth, his eyes darting over many tourists who were being guided towards the cable cars by security guards and plainclothesmen, who Leah presumed were undercover cops or Pytheon agents.

"Listen to me, you piece of shit. Did you really think you could threaten me, threaten my woman, and I'd let you get away with that? I am going to hunt you down and, when I find you, you're going to beg me for a bullet. I will not back down. I will not back away. I will chase you as long as I have breath and if something happens to me then Pytheon will chase you until someone puts a bullet between your eyes." Seth's voice was as cold as an Arctic snowstorm and as hard as tungsten.

"Congratulations, asshole, you are now Pytheon enemy number one. You're a walking dead man."

Seth ripped the microphone from Ben's vest and destroyed the device under the heel of his shoe. He watched as fake-Ben sank to his knees and started to cry, big, desolate tears running down his face. Leah, unable to watch his anguish, wrapped her head in her arms and bent over at the waist. It was finally over and she couldn't stop shaking.

Seth dropped to his haunches beside her, his breath on the top of her head.

"Leah, it's over." Seth placed his big hand on her head

but she refused to uncurl herself and tears rolled out of her eyes into the crook of her elbow.

"Babe, you're safe." Seth stated, his hand drawing big circles on her back.

"Are you okay?" she demanded, her voice muffled.

"I'm good. You?"

"Just peachy," Leah muttered as she allowed Seth to help her sit up and she placed her elbows on her bended knees.

She couldn't look behind her. She didn't want to see Ben's anguish. She could hear his muffled sobs and that was enough.

"He's in such pain." Leah looked into Seth's eyes and felt the panic recede. "I don't want anything to happen to him."

Seth's mouth was a flat, grim line in his face. "He shoved a gun into you, he threatened to shoot you!"

Leah shook her head. "He did it on The Recruiter's orders, hoping he'd have a change in heart about killing his daughter. He knows his daughter is probably dead, I don't want him to live with that and have to deal with jail."

Seth rubbed a hand over his face. "Shit, Leah."

"He did what he could to protect his daughter. I don't want him punished for that. He could've shot me, could've shot you, but he didn't. Please, Seth, help him."

Seth muttered an oath but she saw the capitulation in his eyes, knew he'd honor her request. "And will you try and find his daughter?" She pushed.

"I will."

Leah turned her head and kissed the ball of his shoulder. "Do you think he's still up here, somewhere on the mountain?"

Seth looked around. "Oh, yeah, he's here, though we'll never know who he is and what he looks like."

"You need to catch this bastard Seth."

Seth helped her up and gathered her to his chest. "That's the plan, angel."

Epilogue

"TELL ME YOU love me. Just once."

"You know damn well that I do."

Leah, sitting in a secluded corner on her veranda—out of sight and just able to hear the chaos in her house—remembered Seth's words and told herself, for the three hundredth and second time in the twenty-four hours since she'd left the mountain, he didn't mean them, that he'd said them under duress.

She'd been kidnapped and her life was under threat, of course he'd give her a dying wish. It was just a kind gesture on his part, a couple of words to give her strength, to send her on her way with.

He didn't mean them. Seth hadn't really changed his mind about her, about them and, if she'd managed to have five minutes alone with him, she would've asked him to clarify that life changing statement.

But time alone with him was something in short supply. Since leaving the mountain, her house had been turned into a mini-Pytheon command base, filled with agents and operatives and law enforcement officials. There was so much testosterone wafting about she thought she should check for hair growing on her chest. Computers littered her dining room table, everyone talked in acronyms and code and Seth, apart from bundling her into a shower and into bed, and shoving a sleeping pill down her throat, hadn't talked to her at all.

He was so regretting his words on the mountain. Leah had to let him go, had to allow him to go back to New York and continue his search for The Recruiter. Someone had to stop him and it looked like Seth was the man. And catching that smart bastard needed someone equally smart, equally determined. Seth, again. But if he were to succeed then he'd have to be totally focused, totally committed. There would be no space for a woman in his life, no time for a relationship.

He'd have to withdraw, retreat, be the lone wolf he was so good at being. Catching The Recruiter was important, it was *essential*, so she'd just have to suck it up. But, God, it hurt.

Leah felt the broad hand on her head and looked up to see Seth standing next to her lounger. His hair was all over the place and he looked exhausted, utterly played out.

"Hi." She moved her legs sideways to make space for him to sit with her on the lounger. She patted the cushion and sighed when Seth's hip pressed into her legs and his hand rested on her thigh.

"I was just thinking about you," Leah softly said.

"I haven't stopped thinking about you," Seth replied, his hand tightening on her thigh. "Are you okay?"

Leah nodded. "Sure. I have questions though."

Seth managed a small smile. "I would be surprised if you

didn't."

"Okay…" Leah lifted her chin towards the dining room. "When do I get my house back?"

"In about five minutes. The last of my guys is clearing out. We've done all we can do here. They need to get back to New York." Seth picked up the glass of red wine on the table next to her and took a sip.

Translation—he had to get back to New York.

"Where is fake-Ben now?"

"In jail," Seth answered and lifted up his hand to stop her from speaking. "He had to go to jail, Leah, he pulled a gun on you and threatened not only you but a lot of tourists. Stone is negotiating with the police and the prosecutors, advising them of the special circumstances that made him do what he did. Stone will get a deal for him but he will spend some time in jail."

Seth continued to speak. "After a lot of questioning, we're satisfied that fake-Ben does not know The Recruiter and that they never met. All their communications were done via throw-away phones and fake email addresses."

Leah looked off into the distance. "And The Recruiter was definitely on the mountain with us?"

Seth nodded. "The listening device was ineffective from a distance so he had to be up there to communicate. Besides, he has a huge ego. He set up this elaborate plan and he would've wanted to see it through. I'm pretty sure he watched everything go down and he was giving instructions as the situation developed."

"So The Recruiter is still in the wind," Leah said, her

voice bleak.

Seth nodded. "Still in the wind."

"Am I still in danger?" Leah asked.

"Jett and I spent forty-five minutes on Skype talking to Sam and Stone about that possibility. We don't think so, angel. He saw me as a threat but, as I told him, it's no longer just me; everyone at Pytheon has vowed to take him down. My fight is their fight and you are no more in danger than anyone else. We think he's retreated back to his swamp and will keep his head down for a while."

"But he won't stop."

Seth's expression hardened. "No."

Seth took a deep breath and Leah cocked her head. What now? She didn't know how much more she could handle. She wasn't used to being threatened and being used as bait and she was done.

"I'm proud of you, sweetheart. You handled yourself, stayed strong and you didn't panic. You are definitely your father's daughter and your brother's sister."

Okay, that what a kick ass compliment!

"You can handle anything, Leah." Seth's steady gaze put starch into her spine and courage into her heart. "So you can, and will, handle this as well. I got word about ten minutes ago that they found Hope's body, in a ditch just outside of New Orleans. The bastard must have given the order to make her suffer and then kill her. Someone followed his orders to the nth degree."

Leah bit her bottom lip. "I'm so sorry." A tear spilled onto her lashes and Seth wiped it away with the pad of his thumb. "Poor fake-Ben, poor Hope."

Seth gripped the bridge of his nose with his finger and thumb. "We're going to get him, angel. I promise you, we will."

Leah's hand drifted over his bent head. "I absolutely believe you will."

Leah watched as Seth gave her a long up and down look, as if he were reassuring himself that she was unhurt. "I'm okay, Seth." she told him.

Seth hauled in a deep breath. "I know but I need constant reassurance. Every time I remember how close you came to dying—which is every five fucking minutes—I have to look at you, find you, remind myself that you are fine. It'll be a while before I stop doing that."

"You don't have a while! You have to stop thinking about me and what we went through if you're going to chase down that psycho. You need to focus and focus damn hard because if you get hurt, I'll shoot you myself!"

Seth lifted his head and frowned at her agitation. "What are you talking about?"

"You're going to hunt The Recruiter and he won't like being hunted."

"No, I'm not, I'm not going anywhere. Stone has agreed to setting up a Pytheon task force, which I'll oversee. Jett will be chasing down leads, crisscrossing the world to track The Recruiter."

"And what will you be doing?" Leah demanded.

"Going to work every day, coming home to you every night, making love to you every day." Seth lifted his head to look at her and Leah saw the love he found so difficult to express in his eyes. "I need to get back to New York and I'm really hoping that you'll come with me.

"I can't walk away from Pytheon, Leah, not yet. I would be thrilled if you moved back to the States to be with me but if you can't see yourself doing that then we'll do the long distance, fly over when we can option, at least until that bastard is caught. Then I can, I think, move on, do something else. I'm battling with the idea of leaving Pytheon but I'm willing to consider the possibility. I'd do anything for you Leah...*anything.*"

Leah blinked, her eyes owl wide. His words were in English but they made as much sense as Farsi.

Seth snapped his fingers in front of her face to break her astounded stare. "You with me, angel?"

"You want me? With you?" Leah asked, her voice laced with insecurity.

He swiped his thumb across her full, trembling, bottom lip. "Always."

"Then you meant what you said, on the mountain?"

"That I love you? Of course I meant that. Why would you think otherwise?"

Leah managed a small laugh. "I thought you said it under duress, because of the situation."

Seth wound his arm around Leah's waist and in one easy movement pulled her on to his lap. He buried his face in her hair. "I meant every word. I love you, I always will." He said, his voice vibrating with an emotion she thought she'd never hear. "I was so damn scared I'd lose you."

Leah turned her head to kiss his throat. "I'm not that easy to lose. I love you, too, in case you were wondering."

Leah watched as the last of his reservations, his fears about a relationship disappeared from his eyes. Together they could do anything, be anything, experience everything. "You are my heartbeat, Leah. You are the place my soul looks for when I need peace. And faith. And hope."

Leah wrapped her arm around his neck and held him close. She inhaled his scent and, for the first time in her life, her heart felt safe.

Leah tipped her head back and she saw her happiness reflected in her eyes. She knew it would follow them for the rest of their lives.

"So, hotshot, what you doing for the rest of your life?" she asked, laughter coating her words.

Her lover's cocky smile made her heart flip over. "You, sweetheart. I'm doing you."

The End

The Pytheon Security Series

Book 1: *Claimed by the Warrior*
Jed Hamilton's story

Book 2: *His Toughest Call*
Seth Halcott's story

Available now at your favorite online retailer!

About the Author

Joss Wood's passion for putting black letters on a white screen is only matched by her love of books and travelling (especially to the wild places of Southern Africa) and, possibly, by her hatred of ironing and making school lunches.

After juggling a career in business lobbying and economic development with writing, and somehow managing to produce sixteen books, Joss now spends her days creating contemporary fairy tales. She lives in Kwazulu-Natal, South Africa with her husband and two children surrounded by family, friends, animals and a ridiculous amount of reading material.

Thank you for reading

His Toughest Call

If you enjoyed this book, you can find more from all our great authors at TulePublishing.com, or from your favorite online retailer.

Made in the USA
San Bernardino, CA
24 February 2018